The Headmaster's
Tenure Just Expired . . .

Walter looked up. There was a light at one of the second-floor windows. He counted; third from the end. That was the little anteroom to Salgo's office. Had he left the light on? Why hadn't he noticed? But he must have. He was getting old, he thought. Old and tired. Well, the school could just pay the extra pennies for a change. There was no way he was going back in there tonight. It was just too damn cold, and he needed to get himself home.

He passed beneath an old pin oak, whose skeletal form still held a few stubborn leaves. Its shape blotted the building from view, and so Walter didn't see the shadow that crossed in front of the uncurtained window above . . .

MORE MYSTERIES FROM THE BERKLEY PUBLISHING GROUP . . .

A Dewey James Mystery

THE OLD SCHOOL DIES

Kate Morgan

BERKLEY PRIME CRIME, NEW YORK

THE OLD SCHOOL DIES

A Berkley Prime Crime Book / published by arrangement with the author

PRINTING HISTORY
Berkley Prime Crime edition / November 1996

The Putnam Berkley World Wide Web site address is http://www.berkley.com

ISBN: 0-425-15552-8

Berkley Prime Crime Books are published by The Berkley Publishing Group, 200 Madison Avenue, New York, NY 10016.
The name BERKLEY PRIME CRIME and the BERKLEY PRIME CRIME design are trademarks belonging to Berkley Publishing Corporation.

PRINTED IN THE UNITED STATES OF AMERICA

10 9 8 7 6 5 4 3 2 1

1

IN HIS OAK-PANELED office in the Blair Building of the Jefferson School, Victor Salgo was daydreaming again. He leaned back in his custom-made leather chair, which over the course of two years had shaped itself perfectly to his pyriform body, and stared up at the ornate, vaguely Art Nouveau plaster molding of the ceiling. There were patterns in the molding—nothing fixed, but subject to interpretations as various as the moods of the observer; in two years, Salgo had discerned in the amorphous blobs above his head everything from dancing elephants to sailboats to the faces of the grimmest demons. Today, he was seeing sailboats again, and a beautiful beach, and clear aquamarine water, coral reefs, tall cool rum drinks, and tall cool women. He was seeing islands in the Caribbean—

but the fierce, strident shriek of the bell brought him back to earth.

A look at his watch told him it was ten-thirty; he braced himself for the roar that would follow. Morning recess: The students began streaming from their classrooms like prisoners who find their cell doors suddenly ajar, fiercely jubilant even in the face of certain recapture.

He knew how they must feel.

A glance out the window showed that the day had not improved: gray, cold, with a promise of a cold rain to come. To Salgo, the weather was a perfect reflection of life. It was the first Monday after Thanksgiving, and the burden of the Hamilton winter was settling in already. This was always the busiest part of the school year, with a flurry of faculty and administrative activity before the end of term, which would be crammed in just before the winter vacation. Two short weeks off would be followed by the heaviness of January, the dreariness of February, the long haul to the spring break. Along the way they would encounter endless evenings of student concerts, parent-teacher meetings, and college-guidance sessions. In other words, interminable hours of make-nice, smiley-smiley PR for the headmaster of the Jefferson School, Victor Salgo.

Once again he puzzled over his decision to take this job. He'd been much better off as a teacher—he'd spent five pretty good years in the math department, where nobody bothered him, and he'd found a way to get everything he wanted. Even as department head, he'd had freedom and been able to keep a pretty low profile, do what he wanted. The low profile suited him, because he wasn't much good at warming to the public. Nor did they particularly warm to him.

He had found out that being the headmaster of the Jefferson was demanding and different. It hadn't taken him long to figure out that the Jefferson—with its sticky overlay of tradition, with its prickly Board of Trustees, and its seemingly indomitable uprightness—was too much of a head trip. He wanted more out of life. The very prestige of the place weighted him down like a damp overcoat in a stuffy room, or cement overshoes.

Salgo paused in his meditations, putting on his James Cagney face. You dirty rat. Or was that Edward G. Robinson?

He certainly was no Mr. Chips.

Ye gods, the complaints! First the teachers— well, he knew the salaries were bad, but that was education. What did they expect? They ought to plan, like he did. Then the parents— Why wasn't Sally chosen for the lead in the class play? Little Freddy needs *special* motivation, please be sure to tell his teacher never to leave his side during class. What do you mean young Horace is on the bench? The Wilburton men have *always* played first-string on the varsity, young man. Don't you have any sense of tradition?

And of course the ever-loving Public at Large. The latest headache had been the Greater Hamilton Community Board, whose members were raising a huge stink about an easement that had been breached by the construction of the new fence around the lower athletic field. If the school hadn't put up a fence, they would no doubt have heard from the Public Safety Board or the Zoning Commission instead.

And just this morning he had learned that the Parent-Teacher Community Coordinating Committee was up in arms about something. They were always up in arms. Salgo figured half the committee members didn't have enough to do; sat around all day dreaming up problems for themselves.

God, there was no pleasing some people.

He wished he'd never accepted the job. He had plenty of money—he had a knack for arranging things, he supposed, because it had all worked out nicely. And of course he had inherited a little cash from his parents. He had taken up teaching because he'd been offered a job by the father of a friend, back in New York City. And then, when things had gotten uncomfortable, he'd applied to a couple of schools out of state. Taking a job at the prestigious Jefferson had been an easy step.

Ten years back East had been enough; he didn't care if he never ate another $300 dinner, never went to another art gallery or prestigious museum, never rode another subway. Well, he would miss the Chinese food in New York. But the little coffee shop here in town was a better joint for breakfast and lunch than you could find these days in most places, what with all the old corner coffee shops gone the way of the dinosaur. You wanted plain pancakes with sausage in the city, you had to pay big for it at some artsy place, and be stared at by a lot of art directors in black jackets and ponytails. Victor Salgo had seen enough of that kind of thing to last him a lifetime.

He had liked Hamilton at first. People were friendly enough, not too pushy or nosy. He'd come here in his Beamer because he liked horses and horse country, liked the good life, and didn't particularly mind small-town living. There were some cute women around, although not as many now as there had been ten years ago. Well, that was what happened to women: They got old. Then the young ones didn't even give you a look. He didn't care too much, anyway. There was always someone around; he liked having a clean slate from time to time, but it always got written on again.

Lately, however, Hamilton had gotten to be a bore, and going administrative had been a big mistake. He'd thought it would be amusing for him, Victor Salgo, to be head of the oh-so-mighty Jefferson School, but he never figured on the headaches. Hell, he should've been a shrink or a lawyer, charged by the hour to listen to people complain.

The worst part was the feeling that they all gave him—the trustees, the parents, everyone—that he wasn't good enough. Of course he had to admit he wasn't *one · of them*. Not that he wanted to be. But still.

Young Horace is a Wilburton, by God. Six generations of Wilburtons at the Jeff. Six.

Well, then, why the hell had they offered him the job of headmaster in the first place? He had a sneaking suspicion that it was somehow connected with redressing ethnic imbalances of the past. Hell, he'd always figured history was history, you live in the present. On the other hand he didn't mind making misconceptions work to his advantage. He knew that Rigton Blair, chairman of the Board of Trustees, assumed he was Hispanic. Just because of his last name, the stupid old geezer. Always asking him about Mexico and Venezuela, as though Salgo gave a damn.

Now, on this rainy Monday in late November, Victor Salgo had had it. He was ready to split, take off for a hot island with cool rum drinks and cool women. He was tired of the charade, the politeness, the endless gratitude and platitudes and school spirit. He just wasn't cut out for this kind of— He was getting ready to resign. He had it all worked out. The Jefferson School could take its traditions and its complainers and its moralizing and find someone else to put up with all the— But first, there was one small thing he wanted to do. He had an idea about something. Maybe he could make his mark, and then depart. Future generations of Jeffersonians would thank him. Maybe. But even if they didn't, he'd have put in his two cents.

George Farnham had been cursed by a heavy-handed Providence with a keen mind, an equable temper, a civic conscience, and an unfailingly polite manner. These attributes had damned him to years of servitude on committees, councils, boards, and decision-making teams. Unfortunately, George Farnham loathed discussion groups of any kind—loathed them as much as they desired his participation. Alas, his conscience and sense of duty nearly always won out over personal inclination. Thus the town of Hamilton had taken steady advantage of his willingness throughout the years, the good mothers and fathers and neighbors somehow prevailing on him to help with this fundraiser or that community problem. A level-headed lawyer, a widely respected citizen, a friend to all and sundry, Farnham rarely quarreled with his fellow committee members, never made his arguments personal, and had somehow miraculously developed the knack of getting his suggestions through without ruffling feathers.

It was no wonder, then, that the Board of Trustees of the Jefferson School had seized upon him in their hour of need. Faced with a member's sudden withdrawal, the board had shanghaied George, telling him it would be a piece of cake—and temporary, to boot. After all, the biggest difficulty the board usually faced was finding ways to spend the Jefferson's sizable endowment. George, with his fine sense of diplomacy, would have everyone agreeing and feeling good in no time flat. And there were never any problems at the Jeff, they pointed out.

No, there really never had been—until now.

When George Farnham, in answer to an emergency summons, entered the Faculty Conference Room at the school, he was greeted by a babble of voices rising to near hysterical pitch. Taking a seat at the huge old mahogany table, he listened to the controversy raging around him. Finally Rigton Blair called the meeting to order.

"As this is an emergency session, we'll dispense with reading the minutes from the last meeting—"

"We can't do that!" objected Sandra Albee, the recording secretary. Sandra always relished the few moments when she had the full attention of the board. She wrote excellent minutes, with just the twist of superiority and criticism necessary to make people nervous. "We can't dispense with them."

"Thank you, Mrs. Albee. We can and we will." Blair's tone was full of rebuke, and Sandra backed off, with the calculating air of someone saving her strength for a fight that really mattered.

"Now," continued Blair in his crusty old voice, "the purpose of this meeting is merely to appraise the board of a certain, er, unpleasantness that we are facing." He held up a piece of paper. George could see that it was a letter. "I regret to inform you that this piece of writing concerns our present headmaster, Mr. Salgo." The group was all attention. "Allegations of a most unpleasant and disturbing nature have surfaced."

"Allegations? Or rumors?" asked Tony Zimmerman.

Blair peered over his half-glasses with annoyance. "You lawyers are all the same. Just listen to the damn thing, Tony."

The room grew suddenly quiet. This was what everyone had come for. The dirt on Victor Salgo was about to be dished up—and with Rigton Blair's silver spoon, no less. George looked around at the faces—some only expectant, others almost salivating with anticipation. He had the sinking feeling that he was about to witness the end of a man's career.

"The thing is not dated," said Blair. "It is typewritten and contains neither heading nor address. It reached me yesterday. 'Dear Mr. Blair,' it says. 'I think you should know that the man in charge of the Jefferson School is a thief and worse. Why do you think he is hiding out in Hamilton? If you want details, I am sure that you are prepared to pay. I will call you next week to discuss the cost of the proof.' It is, of course, unsigned, "Blair said.

"That's it?" asked someone.

"Throw it away," suggested another.

"Where there's smoke—" insisted a predictable third.

George Farnham sat back. He had never heard anything so lame in his life.

The only remarkable thing was that Rigton Blair had wanted the trustees to hear it.

Which undoubtedly meant that he had an agenda. There could be little doubt what Rigton Blair was after—the removal of Victor Salgo from the school. Absently, George began to wonder why.

2

IN THE FROSTY light of the late December afternoon, the darkened hallway had the gloomy aspect that all school buildings acquire when there are no children present. The green-on-green speckled linoleum, scuffed by countless heels, had no luster; the doors and doorsills bore forlorn smudges and dents and various other marks. The long corridor, with its sallow, dough-colored walls, was decked out with multicolored didactic posters advertising the fun of reading and the dangers of drugs; in the semi-darkness, the colors were muted, and the posters seemed pointless and sad.

Walter Hartung, methodically sweeping up mountains of paper, candy wrappers, soft-drink cans, and the other detritus of teenage living, whistled tunelessly. He was accustomed to seeing the Jefferson School this way; the absence of the children didn't strike him as inappropriate. In fact, at his age and in his line of work, he preferred things this way.

Even when school was in session, the students and Walter gave each other a wide berth. You couldn't blame the students for keeping their distance, for even in the days before his rheumatism had made him crabby, Walter Hartung had hardly been the type of kindly old school custodian you might find in the pages of *My Weekly Reader*. Walter had never had much use for kids. The best of them were usually noisy and sloppy; the rest were inconsiderate or downright unkind. They were just like grownups, in other words, without the window-dressing that most of them eventually acquire.

The teachers were the same, in Walter's book. They always had some mess or other for him to clean up. As chief custodian, Walter was the one they called when someone broke a chair, or put a hole through a window, or spilled the dreadful contents of a biology experiment. He supposed they were nice enough about it, but he wished they'd learn to mop up their own messes.

The secretaries and the administrators were the ones who really took the cake. Most of them never spoke to him; the only one who did always flashed a smile that was enough to turn his stomach, it was so full of condescension. He never smiled back at her. He had enough dirt on her to fill a book.

Walter and his staff were always especially busy at the end of term or when it rained for long periods of time. Rain made the kids worse than ever. He knew from experience that on a day like today—the last Friday before the winter vacation, after a week of freezing rain—he could expect the worst. This semester, as usual, had finished with a flurry of exams and papers and parties and pageants. The classrooms in Tyson Hall had been piled high with trash and carelessly discarded clothes; in the corners and under chairs were half-eaten Christmas cookies and gingerbread men and other choice leftovers.

Absent-mindedly he pushed up the sleeves of his dark blue overall and bent to his task. He would finish sweeping this hallway, and then do the wastebaskets in the administration building. That would be enough for today. He felt tired; it was late. After that last scare, he needed to pace himself. The worst of the classrooms could wait until tomorrow, when the rest of the custodial staff would be here to help.

When he got to the enclave of offices surrounding the principal's lair, he found that the grownups hadn't been much neater than the students. The two front-office secretaries had evidently made some effort to tidy up, but they hadn't succeeded. Probably they had been exhausted by the overwhelming task of collating the exams, printing out the report cards, sending out the Honor Roll letters, and putting everything in order for the coming semester. Walter knew it took a lot of work to finish it all; the job had been made harder by the terrible fuss that had been raging today, following the sudden departure of Victor Salgo, Jefferson's headmaster.

Walter hadn't been sorry to hear that he had left; no one had. In his brief career at Jefferson, Salgo had made dozens of enemies among the teachers, parents, trustees, custodians—just about everyone associated with the school. His manner had been abrasive, his demands on the staff—including Walter—excessive. Walter was glad he was gone.

The students, in one of those predictable ironies of school life, had rather liked Salgo, perhaps because he was a born troublemaker. He had about him the air of someone with a string of demerits and detentions: someone whose bad report card followed him through life. Walter had seen in Salgo's eyes the same look that the kids wore when they had to come in on Saturday for detentions. Smirking, smart-alecky. Salgo had probably chosen a career in education administration to get back at his old teachers. He had been on the warpath from the word go; Walter, making his quiet way from one corner of the school to another, was always in a position to know. He overheard a great deal, one way or another. There was a lot he could have told people, had anyone bothered to ask him. It was typical of the Jeff, of course, that nobody did.

Walter wondered who they would get to replace Salgo. At this time of year it would be hard; Leticia Sanderson had of course been appointed Acting Head; but she had made a lot of enemies over the years, and her chances of winning the job permanently, Walter figured, were about a thousand to one—unless she pulled a fast one.

As Walter emptied the wastebaskets into the large trash barrel, the image of the doughty Mrs. Sanderson floated before him. She was a smug little beetle of a woman, unfriendly, rigid, with an ambition as big as all outdoors and a bosom to match. She had started out as the receptionist in the little front office, gradually moving up within the administrative ranks. It was common knowledge that she had never, since her student days, seen the inside of a classroom. Somehow that hadn't stopped her.

In the late seventies she had benefited from a sudden fever of permissiveness that had swept through the school board; despite her near-total lack of credentials, she had been promoted to Supervisor for Student Affairs. In that job she had been mainly expected to keep the school dances free from pot and beer, but Leticia, putting on airs and posturing and jousting with the staff, had somehow made her new job into a focus of power; and in the last ten years she had made herself stronger still. Walter forgot what her most recent title had been; the faculty and staff always had a nickname for her. Lately she had been known as the Power Mother.

Even if she was a Power Mother, Walter Hartung wasn't afraid of her. He was the only person who had been at Jefferson longer than Leticia. He figured he had her number, more or less. They'd had plenty of run-ins over the years as Leticia made her unladylike way up the administrative ladder.

It looked as though the Power Mother was going to do it again, Walter reflected. With typically crude haste she had already moved her things into Salgo's office, staking out her territory. Walter, as he righted the furniture and dusted the bookshelves, recognized a moth-eaten philodendron, an ancient poster of Albert Einstein, and a copy of *Cultural Literacy* as lately having been in her small cubicle down the hall.

He emptied the wastebasket and shut the door behind him, with a shake of his head. Though he was the last person to be sentimental about his place of employment, Walter Hartung felt a small twinge of foreboding. It would change the course of the school's history if that woman had her way. Walter wasn't a snob, and he had but small affection for the school. But he knew the Jeff would never be the same again if Leticia's appointment became permanent.

Limping slightly, he wheeled the big trash barrel from the administration building to the fancy new Hertz Science Laboratory, where the custodians had been granted a small cellar room for their needs. The room, little better than a cell, its yellow cinder-block walls already showing the dirt, was furnished for the janitors' convenience with broken desks and dented lockers that didn't shut. With a grunt, Walter set down his broom, changed out of his blue overall, pulled on his parka, and switched off the light. He had done enough for today.

He went out through the main gate and headed for the staff parking lot out on Melrose Avenue, turning up his collar against the cold. His bad knee was giving a lot of pain tonight, and there was an icy wind blowing from the north. He made slow progress as he took the shortcut across the deserted athletic field. In the darkness, the hulk of the Blair Building, sitting atop a small hill, loomed menacingly. Once a private home on a large estate, it had served as the Jefferson's administration building for eighty years. It was connected to the newer buildings by a series of enclosed porticos that wound beneath the copper beeches and tall hemlocks that graced the grounds.

Walter looked up. There was a light at one of the second-floor windows. He counted; third from the end. That was the little anteroom to Salgo's office. Had he left the light on? Why hadn't he noticed? But he must have. He was getting old, he thought. Old and tired. Well, the school could just pay the extra pennies for a change. There was no way he was going back in there tonight. It was just too damn cold, and he needed to get himself home.

He passed beneath an old pin oak, whose skeletal form still held a few stubborn leaves. Its shape blotted the building from view, and so Walter didn't see the shadow that crossed in front of the uncurtained window above.

3

"WELL, HONESTLY, GEORGE," exclaimed Dewey James. "I do think we had better be careful. That woman gets everything she wants. From what I've heard, she'll be headmistress before long."

"Don't know why you particularly care, my dear," replied George Farnham abstractedly, accepting a cup of fresh coffee. He was seated in a comfortable pinewood chair; on the antique cherry table was a copy of the *Quill*, the local weekly newspaper. Side-by-side photos of Leticia Sanderson and Victor Salgo occupied a quarter of the front page, under the headline HEADMASTER'S HASTY DEPARTURE SPELLS TOUGH TIMES FOR THE JEFF.

George gazed out the kitchen window and sipped his coffee. Outside, the air was bright with a frosty winter light. From where he sat he could see the small pasture where Dewey's mare, Starbuck, liked to graze in the summer. The grass had gone brown and hard with the recent frost, and there were patches of mud here and there. Still, the sweeping view across the countryside from Dewey's house to the top of Adams Hill was impressive. When the spring came again it would be beautiful.

George loved to sit here with Dewey, admiring the view and speculating about local affairs. Lately, this coffee klatch in Dewey's kitchen had become a Saturday-morning ritual for the two old friends. George welcomed the coziness of their new tradition, both for its tranquility and for the promise of ever-deepening friendship.

Dewey's kitchen had remained basically unchanged since she and her late husband, Brendan, had bought the house during the first years of their marriage. The table was old, sturdy, and well-worn; the painted pine chairs had gingham-covered cushions that matched the mended curtains at the window. In one corner was a small cherry bookcase holding falling-apart cookbooks and a jumble of family memorabilia—pictures of Dewey's daughter, Grace, now grown and living in San Diego; an old Hamilton Hornets baseball cap; a photo of Brendan James in his prime, shortly after his promotion to captain of the Hamilton Police Department. Scattered here and there were dozens of the little doodads that families acquire on their adventures: their camping trips and excursions to New York City, Hershey Park, Yosemite, the World's Fair, and the Kentucky Derby. In Dewey James's kitchen, George Farnham felt utterly at home, as he had for many years.

He glanced down at the headline in the *Quill*. A pitched battle seemed to be in the offing. George wanted no part of it; but he knew it would be difficult for most townspeople to keep their opinions to themselves. Some might even be prompted to take action, one way or another.

Like small towns everywhere, Hamilton had its little dramas and scandals, most of which passed unnoticed by the larger world outside. Visitors to the peaceful little valley were content to admire the two rushing rivers, the scattered stands of ancient trees, and the neatly groomed pastureland where champion Thoroughbreds were raised. Only occasionally did true unpleasantness erupt; only rarely were news teams, complete with minicams, summoned to bear witness to dreadful goings-on. But to Dewey, the adventures of her neighbors were always a source of great interest; she considered herself a student of human nature. George leaned his elbows comfortably on the table and prepared to debate.

"The Jeff's a great school, but it's not as though you or I have children there." He glanced at the photo of Salgo. Had he not been flabby, the former headmaster would have been attractive, with the slick handsomeness of a soap-opera bad guy, or a political candidate of questionable morals. Make that, *ipso facto*, a political candidate, George reflected cynically, returning his attention to the conversation. "You must know that it's really nobody's business but the school's."

"I know." Dewey nodded, her silver-gray curls shining in the morning sunlight. "Although with luck I may one day be a grandmother to a Jefferson boy or girl. No—" she waved a half-buttered piece of toast in the air, "I know I haven't got a legitimate voice in school affairs, or anything. But honestly, George, that woman does not have a single qualification. Not one." Dewey pointed at the photo of Leticia Sanderson. "She is not suited to take charge of the Jefferson."

George tended to agree, but he sensed that Dewey was getting ready to mount a campaign. He wasn't inclined to encourage his friend's would-be activism. In Hamilton, Dewey James had long been famous for Stirring Things Up. The search for a new head for the Jefferson—a nationally prestigious institution and the source of a certain amount of local pride—would be certain to create a swirl of ill feeling and recriminations such as the town hadn't seen in years. George, although a Jefferson alumnus and a temporary trustee, didn't intend to become any more involved than should prove absolutely necessary. The school was now obliged to make up for its dreadful mistake in having hired Salgo in the first place. The trustees would have to be especially careful right now; George was not at all sure that Leticia Sanderson could manipulate the board. Once burned, twice learned.

But even if she won the position, nobody could be as bad for the Jefferson as Victor Salgo had been. Anyone would be an improvement. Even Leticia Sanderson.

George voiced this sentiment to Dewey.

"Naturally. A rhesus monkey would be an improvement," Dewey agreed, offering him a jar of gooseberry jam for his toast. "But that's beside the point. The thing is this: Do we simply want to do better than that awful creature? Or do we want the right kind of person in the job?"

"Who's 'we'?" asked George, taking a covert sniff of the jam. Things had a way of staying in Dewey's refrigerator for unusually long periods of time, and experience had taught him that it was better to be safe than sorry.

"*We* are. All of us here, George. You know as well as I do that the Jefferson School is vitally important to Hamilton's cultural profile."

George spread some jam on his toast. "Whoa, my dear. You sound like you've been reading some kind of trashy, do-it-yourself civics best-seller."

"I have not." Dewey blushed becomingly. She

always blushed when she lied. It was just the plain facts of the case that in her position as the director of the town's excellent little library— or really, director emeritus, for she was now semiretired—Dewey cast an eye on a good many books that weren't really her kind of thing at all. She was possessed of a naturally curious mind and a strong ability to retain what she had read; fortunately her powers of discrimination served her well.

"We ought just to sit back, my dear, and let the board and the parents resolve it." George took a bite of his toast.

"That's easy for you to say, George. At least you have a voice on the board."

"Not really, my dear. I'm only sitting in until a new permanent member can be appointed in April."

"Your timing is perfect," retorted Dewey, with a twinkle in her eye. She conjured up a mental image of Rigton Blair, the chairman, whose constrained and formal manner was frosty, formidable, and old-fashioned. Dewey recalled seeing Blair at the hardware store shortly after Victor Salgo's ascendancy to the post of headmaster. Blair's habitually impassive expression had given way to a look of extreme discontent; his small gray eyes had borne a look of intensity that Dewey hadn't seen before. Upon greeting him politely, she had been less than politely rebuffed. Salgo's appointment had been a bitter pill for Blair, and everyone in Hamilton knew it.

Today, reflected Dewey, Blair was no doubt celebrating, after the manner of the terminally stuffy, the departure of Victor Salgo. Perhaps he had allowed himself a small smile to mark the occasion. "At least Rigton Blair will feel himself vindicated," Dewey said aloud. "He will be shown to have been right, after all."

"Of course he was right," agreed George. "That will just make him all the more ill-tempered." Through the years George had served on numerous committees with Blair, and he knew whereof he spoke. "He can be downright disagreeable when he's right."

"Aha!" Dewey exclaimed. "You watch, George. He'll make everybody furious, and you'll make an even worse mess of it than before."

"Now, Dewey." George gave his friend an innocent look of wounded pride. "I'm sure we'll do our best. You have to put your faith in something."

"With that autocrat manipulating everyone, and everybody feeling stupid to begin with? You're the only one with an ounce of sense, George, and what can you do?"

"Thank you, my dear," replied George, smiling. "You certainly know how to make a fellow feel good."

"Don't be ridiculous. You know what I mean.

You're wonderful, George, but you're only one person. And I'll just bet you Rigton Blair will come out fighting." She gave it some thought, then brightened. "Maybe he'll retire."

"Hah. Not a chance. Thinks he's the heart and mind and soul of the Jefferson."

"Well, yes. But isn't there a term limit on the board?"

"For the mere mortals, yes. But Rigton Blair, thanks to his generosity past, present and future, was named a Lifetime Appointee."

Dewey rolled her eyes.

"That's right," George went on. "We're stuck with him, my dear. Till he departs this earthly sphere."

"Oh, dear." Dewey finished the last of her coffee. "I'm sure you'll find a way to manage him, George. And speaking of earthly spheres, do you think you could lend me a hand in the garden?"

"Ah, Hamilton's own Gertrude Jekyll. Doing some early planting?" George chuckled.

Dewey was an avid gardener, but she often worked at it with more enthusiasm than success. When people seemed inclined to criticize, she defended her garden's landscape as "naturalistic"; others might have called it simply untended.

"Now, George, there is no need for sarcasm," she replied with great dignity. "I need to mulch the box bushes."

George smiled. "Delighted to help, my dear. Delighted."

"Thank you very mulch," said Dewey, with a twinkle.

4

"DECK US ALL with Boston Charlie! Walla-Walla Wash and Kalamazoo!" Murray Hill's bold baritone was only slightly furred by last night's excesses at the Seven Locks Tavern, where he had been celebrating the end of the long semester and the start of the winter vacation. His voice, vigorous and captivating, soared above the roar of the shower and echoed off the tiled walls of the bathroom. "Nora's freezin' on the trolley! Swaller, dollar, cauliflower, Alley-ga-Roo!"

This morning, Murray was feeling particularly exuberant. He loved the winter in Hamilton. Born and raised in New Orleans, he hadn't known snow, or sleds, or outdoor ice-skating as a child. During his first winter as a teacher at the Jeff, a dozen years ago, he had stumbled upon a whole new world. He had discovered that exquisite feeling in your cheeks when you come in from the cold, the glories of hot chocolate, the unequaled pleasantness of falling asleep over a good book in front of an open fire on a freezing cold day.

His parents and sisters didn't understand. They had made the pilgrimage from New Orleans only once, to spend the Christmas season with him here in Hamilton. They had complained bitterly of the cold, shivering and shaking the entire time, and he had never been able to tempt them back again. For his part, he had renounced the Gulf Coast. He had fallen in love with the changing of the seasons in Hamilton, with fall, winter, and spring—but most of all with winter. He steadfastly refused to go back to Dixie, except for brief visits in the sweltering months of July and August.

He stepped out of the shower, rubbed down quickly with a towel, and gave himself a measuring glance in the mirror. Not bad. Thirty-three, maintaining a respectable head of hair, and bearing less of a paunch than a lot of his office-bound buddies—thanks to being on his feet all day. There wasn't any real money in teaching, of course, but he could live without real money. He loved his work, and he wasn't in any hurry to acquire a mortgage or a fancy car. And when the day came to marry, he would just have to find himself a rich girl. For now, he was pleased with his life.

He had come a long way in twelve years. He was chairman of the Jefferson English department, assistant coach of the Jefferson Blades (four-time regional ice-hockey champs), and a member of the Wolf Tones, a local all-male singing group. The only thing he really missed about New Orleans, aside from pecan waffles at the Camellia Grill, was the oysters. But just last month he had found a seafood company that would ship him a dozen every month by Federal Express.

In short, Murray Hill had begun to feel that his life was more or less perfect. Especially now that vacation was beginning. His vacations were always an idyll of reading and note-taking, of making minor adjustments to the curriculum, of inventing new ways to make the monthly departmental meetings marginally less boring.

Last semester had been especially arduous, because of the gossip that had been flying since Thanksgiving about Victor Salgo. Well, he was gone, that was behind them. It was weird the way Salgo had come and gone, breezing in like Warren Beatty on a good day, then leaving with his tail between his legs, like Danny DeVito hamming it up. It had all been too theatrical for words.

He dressed hurriedly in gray flannels, tweed sports coat, and rep tie. He glanced at his watch—perfect timing. He was due to meet Rigton Blair downtown at the Hamilton Club for coffee and a discussion of the problem the Jeff was now facing.

It took several hours for the weak winter sunlight to penetrate the deeper recesses of Johnson's Ravine. It was a thickly wooded spot, and there was (as the name implied) a fairly steep drop, from the hillside above to the rushing Boone River below. This was one of the rockier spots in the river's course, and through the little gorge at the bottom of the ravine, the river narrowed and picked up speed at the same time. It wasn't a swirling rapids, exactly, but it was different from the way that the Boone meandered lazily along through the agricultural land just a mile or so downriver.

There was just one spot where the sun could break through more clearly, a broad swath of ground that was relatively free of trees, and through here the winter sun reached the bottom of the ravine. On this cold December morning, the darkness at the bottom of the ravine was giving back light. As the sun climbed over the back of the hillside above, an observer would have seen the glint of chrome, the play of light on a bright green fender, the gleam of sunlight reflected by a wide expanse of glass.

But there were no observers—Johnson's Ravine was a deserted spot, a place where no one ventured.

*   *   *

Hill had been to the Hamilton Club on several occasions. This morning, as he mounted the seven wide granite steps and entered the marbled elegance of the foyer, he again experienced the conflicting sensations that accompanied him here. On one level he found it difficult to approve of the club's exclusive atmosphere; but once inside, it was equally difficult to feel at odds with the place. It hailed you as a hero; it saluted your successes and waved aside your failures, making them appear distant, trivial. Once inside, you could believe that you had arrived.

The main lounge, known as the Reading Room, had ancient mahogany wainscoting and faded oil portraits of dead-and-gone civic leaders. The well-worn leather armchairs welcomed you with a soft sigh; the waiters, formal but never superior, were a throwback to another time and place. In their short white jackets they reminded Hill of long-ago train travel.

He had to admit that he liked the Hamilton Club. It was a marvelous experience to sit quietly in the light of one of the large bow windows that looked out across Slingluff Street toward the Boone River, discussing this or that over a drink. In places like this Hill was grateful for his Southern upbringing, which had made good manners a reflex. If you had good manners, you could go anywhere—that was what his daddy had taught him.

The problem was that the club wasn't exactly open in its membership policies, and Murray felt that, given his own overtly liberal political ideals, he shouldn't condone the existence of such places. But Murray Hill wasn't about to ask the Jefferson board chairman to meet him someplace else. Besides, this was probably the only place in town that Rigton Blair knew how to find. This and his barbershop and his office at the headquarters of the Blair National Bank. Rigton Blair didn't get about much; but then, he didn't need to. Generally speaking, the world came to him.

Hill gave his name to the chief steward and was escorted into the Reading Room. Blair was seated in a far corner, his gold-framed glasses low on his nose, a copy of *Barron's* open on his knee. He wore his customary forbidding look, but rose and shook hands, gravely polite, before inviting Hill to take a seat.

"I trust you know why you're here," said Blair, after ordering a pot of coffee and a basket of croissants. He smoothed a trouser leg and made a minute adjustment to his shirt cuff. He didn't wait for a response. "We—the board— are grateful that this deplorable situation has come to an end. Unfortunately, the timing of Salgo's departure leaves much to be desired. He might have had the consideration to finish out the year. We will need the full cooperation of the faculty if we are to get through the coming academic term in proper Jefferson style."

Hill murmured something agreeable, placating. This much he knew already; the whole faculty had been briefed in an emergency meeting Friday morning, just before the start of the Winter Pageant, which was the last activity before vacation. Leticia Sanderson, charged with delivering the news at a hurried session in the faculty lounge, had done her best to keep from gloating, but it had been difficult for her. She had urged the teachers, on behalf of the parents and trustees, not to let their side down. She had gloried in the spotlight and in the power, however transitory, that had been conferred upon her. Then and there Murray Hill had decided to keep as far removed from the situation as possible.

Now Rigton Blair was plonking him right in the middle of everything he detested: politics, rivalries for power, and back-stabbing.

Blair was going on. "In confidence, because we feel that we can trust you, I am going to divulge a small part of what has transpired. I believe I can rely on your discretion."

"Absolutely, sir," replied Hill, feeling like a minor character in a comedy by Sir Arthur Wing Pinero.

"Very well, then. How's your coffee, by the way?"

"Delicious."

"Good. They brew damn good coffee here at the club. Always have, always will."

"Yes, sir." Murray had little doubt that they always would.

"Here is a photocopy of Mr. Salgo's letter to the board." Blair pushed a sheet of paper across the table to Hill. "It is remarkably brief and to the point. Take a look."

Hill picked up the letter and read through it with mild curiosity. The terseness was somewhat surprising. It was dated Thursday evening, a little less than two full days ago.

To Whom It May Concern [the letter began]:

For personal reasons of an urgent and implacable nature, I hereby resign my post as headmaster of the Jefferson School, effective immediately.

Thank you for the opportunity to have served the Jefferson and the Hamilton community.

Respectfully submitted,
[signed] Victor L. Salgo

Hill read it through quickly, then looked up at Blair, who seemed to be expecting some sort of reaction. "You'll note that he doesn't apologize," the chairman prompted.

"No, sir." That had been one of Salgo's maxims—Never Apologize. Hill hadn't understood why Salgo considered it so important; everyone is wrong from time to time. Better just to admit it and go on. Hill pictured Salgo as he had appeared on Thursday morning, during his last assembly before the student body. He had seemed then the picture of complacency. Had he known then that he would be gone in a cloud of disrepute before the next day?

"I imagine he thought that, in the circumstances, it was easiest to be concise," commented Hill finally, handing the letter back. "He always liked that word, 'implacable.'"

"I found it disparagingly brief," Blair replied. "Especially for a man who loves to hear himself talk."

Hill permitted a small smile to cross his face. "Perhaps he finally ran out of things to say."

"Indeed." Rigton Blair cleared his throat. "We've a problem here, of course." He tapped the letter impatiently, folded it, and put it neatly in the breast pocket of his jacket. Hill caught a flash of the label in the jacket: McKean Brothers, Hamilton's only custom tailor. Rigton Blair had probably been wearing that jacket for forty years.

The banker was speaking. "That is, we may have a problem. His contract naturally stipulated that he submit any such letter to the board, and of course he was expected to await our response before leaving. Well." Blair shook his head, a gesture plainly meant to indicate that there was no accounting for some people.

"You will note that this letter is not addressed to the board," Blair went on. "Therefore, according to—according to a board member who is a member of the legal fraternity—there exists the possibility that, should problems arise, this document will not constitute an enforceable letter of resignation."

"Hmm." It was a legal nicety, but Hill took the point.

"In this day and age, Hill, it's damned difficult to get rid of someone once they've got a job." Blair shook his head again. Things Had Been Different in His Day, that was the obvious message. Different and better. "Like leeches, all these damned inefficient freeloaders." He cleared his throat, but to Hill's relief didn't seem to expect an answer. "I'll tell you this much in confidence, young man." He wagged a bony finger at Hill. "The Special Committee had already voted not to renew his contract."

Hill nodded. That wasn't a surprise, nor was it a secret. Vivian the Vivacious—the school's head administrative secretary—had somehow heard about it and told Hill a couple of months back. It was likely that Salgo had known, too, or at least had a sense of it. People generally knew when they were under the gun, and Salgo seemed to have had a streak of paranoia, to boot. An old quip came floating into Hill's brain: "Just because you're paranoid doesn't mean they aren't out to get you." That was definitely true, and the ivy-clad towers of academia seemed to provide cover for an exceptionally efficient class of sniper.

"The problem, as we see it," continued Blair, "is that Salgo could very well turn up all dog-eared in January from a three-week bout in some gin-soaked tavern and demand his old job back. Or worse. I mean, how do we know he hasn't run off to Reno for a quick wedding to some ex-stripper from Baltimore?" He waved his hand dismissively; the ways of lowlifes were out of his orbit.

Hill had to concede the possibility that Salgo might have a change of heart and turn up on January 15. He said as much. "But do you think he will?"

Blair took a swallow of coffee. "Doubtful. Doubtful. But I don't enjoy living with the possibility."

"Has the board considered asking him to submit another, proper letter of resignation?"

"We have," Blair adjusted a gray-flannel trouser leg and took a sip of his coffee. "We could do that. But frankly, I don't want the board to seem to go to him on bended knee. It wouldn't be appropriate."

Hill imagined that it might well be difficult for Blair to approach Salgo in the matter. But didn't the school have a lawyer to look into these things? What about the board member who belonged to the "legal fraternity?"

"Perhaps you understand where I'm headed." Blair fixed Hill with a stern look. "I am sure that you, as a young single man, face only a few of the onerous responsibilities of the Christmas season. My guess is that you find yourself with a fair amount of free time on your hands during the holiday."

"Well—"

"And, frankly, the board needs your help. We have been working on the assumption of your willingness."

"Of course," said Hill, with more enthusiasm than he felt. "You'd like me to talk to him, and ask him to sign another letter."

"Yes. Let him know, tactfully, that we are happy to accept his resignation. Above all I don't want you to do or say anything to change his mind, if this thing" —Blair tapped his breast pocket— "should prove to be unenforceable. It's important for the good of the Jefferson that we have a clear idea of the path that lies before us. It's the merest technicality, I am quite certain—but we would prefer to have that technicality quashed before offering the position to someone new. And I needn't tell you that we will be quite certain, this time, to choose someone who knows that it means to be part of the Jefferson tradition."

Murray Hill was suddenly alert to something

in Blair's voice. There was promise in it that appealed to the young man's sense of accomplishment and to his sense of the possible. He relaxed his shoulders and leaned back in his chair. The well-worn leather let out a soft breath. Here in the Hamilton Club, it was easy to believe in your own success—past, present, and future.

"Whatever I can do, sir, I'll be glad to do," said Hill, using a tone of voice he usually reserved for reading aloud the parts of messengers in Shakespeare's comedies: Biondello, that crowd. He nodded in way that he hoped conveyed a strong sense of duty and accommodation. If any one person could be said to hold the future of the Jeff (and its faculty) in his hands, it was Rigton Blair. "Whatever I can do, sir. Of course." Stark spayed with the spavins, he thought to himself.

"Good, good. We appreciate your help."

"Not at all." Hill wondered if he was dismissed. He glanced at Blair. Not yet, it seemed.

"Now," said the older man, a look of distaste on his elegant face, "I don't suppose you have heard anything about some kind of scandal, or rumor, involving our former head. Have you?"

Blair's abruptly casual tone was in marked contrast to his previous earnestness. Hill was suddenly wary.

"Oh, well, Mr. Blair, you know how schools

are. Rumors fly fast and furious. I try not to listen."

"An excellent habit. But I'm afraid I have to ask you to abandon your principles momentarily, because—and I'm telling you frankly, and in confidence—we have heard rumors, of a sort. In fact, the board received a letter, only two weeks ago, that has puzzled and troubled us. We would very much like to put it all behind us." Blair produced the famous anonymous letter and waited in silence while Hill looked it over.

Hill suddenly understood that his mandate was muckraking. He began to feel uneasy. Digging for dirt wasn't a thing he was particularly good at.

"You'd like me to ask him why he has been characterized as a 'thief and worse'?"

"Well, I very much doubt that he will answer you if you just come right out and ask him." Blair gave Hill a world-weary smile, suddenly transforming himself into a pale imitation of the Edwardian mischief-maker. "But see if you can get a sense of the thing, will you?"

"Um, when you say 'the thing'—does the board have anything more to go on than this? I mean, sir, are there any facts in the case?"

"We're not certain yet. The person who wrote the letter has never contacted us again. Perhaps he or she feels that his mission was satisfactorily concluded." Blair was bankerly again, the teachings of Lord Chesterfield forgotten. "But we are certain that there was some kind of scandal brewing, and there's a chance that some of the dirt may yet be flung our way. I do not intend to sit on pins and needles, waiting for this affair to be tidied up."

Hill doubted that some past scandal in Victor Salgo's life could affect the Jefferson now. But he didn't voice his skepticism. "No, of course not, sir."

"Fortunately, I'm fairly certain all of this has nothing to do with the Jeff," Blair said. "Nonetheless it is an unpleasant matter and it must be cleared up. Cleared up right away." He raised a silvery eyebrow and gave Hill an appraising glance. "The board will consider it a great favor if you can help us, Mr. Hill."

"I'll do my best, sir," said Murray.

On his way home, he gave it some thought. He would talk to Salgo, ask him to sign a more formal letter to the board. He would probe gently on the subject of the anonymous letter. No doubt his inquiries would be met by stony silence, but he would be able to tell Rigton Blair that he had done his downright best. Murray Hill seriously doubted that Victor Salgo would come back to haunt them.

5

Dewey and George's predictions about the level of controversy proved to have been well short of the mark. In Hamilton, where every good citizen bore witness to the smallest changes in the ambient temperature, the people were heating up for a fevered tussle over the newly created vacancy at the Jeff. And nowhere would the strategy of the battle receive more careful, fiercer scrutiny than in the pink and pearly white, perfectly tidy living room of Sandra Albee.

A short, intense-looking woman with baby blue eyes and thin, straight, well-behaved blond hair, Sandra was a born organizer. She was the type who never needed to fear a stranger's prying glance into her sock drawer; in Sandra's world, everything aligned, either by design or because she insisted upon it. She had orchestrated her own life perfectly: She was, at forty-five, well-to-do, with a nice house, fashionable clothes, and a great figure. She had organized her children, now grown, into careers of fair accomplishment and local prominence. Sandra had even organized her pets; the two small dachshunds were tidy and well-groomed, and the cat, a Siamese, was a masterpiece of feline grace and cleanliness.

Sandra had only one blot on her scorecard: Through two and one-half decades of marriage she had utterly failed to organize her husband. For many years he had grudgingly followed the trajectory she had launched him on, all the while silently dreaming of a few days' blessed reprieve from planning. He had finally, half a dozen years ago, taken French leave.

Devastated at first, Sandra decided after a while that it was all the same to her, really; he had always had an unruly streak of spontaneity that made her uncomfortable. Since his departure, she had certainly not lacked for male company. And now that she didn't have to worry about keeping him in line, she had been able to get on with a few things that were important to her. Getting a seat on the prestigious Board of Trustees of the Jefferson School had been just one step on the road to the good life. It was all in who you knew—and what you had in the bank.

Sandra was a model of efficiency when she set

her mind to something. Unfortunately, just as she thought everything had finally been brought under control, a scandal was brewing about who would replace Salgo. It was a situation that needed managing.

Quietly drinking a cup of herbal tea in her living room, Sandra tucked her delicate feet under her and turned her thoughts to dealing with this latest problem at the Jefferson. It usually pleased her to sit quietly in this room; she was soothed by the perfectly matching curtains and upholstery, the flawless carpet, and the tasteful, gleaming mahogany furniture (reproductions, of course—she had always felt that genuine antiques could be unpredictable, and she didn't like the idea of having someone else's furniture). In this room, Sandra Albee always found her values reinforced. She was in control.

Today, however, she found peace elusive. She had been obliged to recognize that the Jefferson's problems, far from being over, were multiplying. So far, the telephone hadn't rung; she hadn't been called in for any hurried conferences with the other trustees, despite the urgency of the situation. Well, after the way she had pushed for Victor Salgo, she could hardly blame the other members of the board for avoiding her. But how was she to have known?

The facts of the case were still obscured by the mists of rumor and half-truths, naturally. A letter the board had recently received from the

Chase School, in New York, where Salgo had worked before coming to the Jefferson, had been disturbing, but very discreet. Well, you had to be discreet in these litigious days—and after all, the facts of the case (if they were facts) were nearly ancient history. But the Chase's very discretion betokened ill. And then there was the matter of the anonymous letter that Rigton Blair had read aloud. It was hardly surprising that the board had wanted Salgo to leave.

And then, of course, there was the girl, the former Chase student who was rumored to be involved somehow in his fall from probity. No doubt, thought Sandra, there had been something going on there. She could always tell.

Salgo's letter of resignation had shed no light on the matter, but that could be construed as natural, too, in the circumstances. If appearances were to be believed, he had simply decided to cut his losses and go. His letter of resignation had cited merely "personal reasons of an urgent and implacable nature." But even if his departure hadn't raised suspicions, the bad odor that would follow him throughout the course of the Chase investigation would have been enough to sink the reputation of a place like the Jeff. It was evident that, one way or another, Victor Salgo had been on his way out.

Sandra glanced at her well-manicured nails. The pale pink polish went perfectly with the pink flowers in a vase atop the mantelpiece.

Funny she hadn't noticed that before. She usually noticed these things. Maybe she was losing it.

Nor had she noticed anything really off about Salgo; that he had turned out to be less than upright had surprised her. But she had to admit that she had found him attractive, right up to the very end. She conjured up an image of him—a little out of shape but still good-looking, a man who knew how to have a good time. He wasn't really the headmasterish type, but there had been something that appealed to that gang of stiff old bores who sat on the school board.

Sandra comforted herself with the thought that it was impossible to have foreseen the problem. No matter how well prepared you were, it was futile to try to anticipate such a turn of events. How could it be her fault?

Unfortunately, Sandra had been the first member of the board to support his application for the job. She remembered how pleased she had been with herself, how persuasively and how credibly she had argued, winning the others over, one by one, and finally claiming the majority vote, stifling once and for all the stolid objections of Rigton Blair.

Well, that hadn't been too difficult, really. That pompous old windbag had gone on and on about Tradition, as though there were only one kind of tradition in life. As though he were the standard-bearer for Dignity, anointed by some connoisseur-on-high to pass judgment on the people around him. Sandra had no use for people who revered the status quo for its own sake. The status quo had never done much for her.

Sandra detested Rigton Blair. He was a self-satisfied old fool, but she didn't hate him merely for that. He was a snob, and unlike Sandra he had not gotten where he was in life by working for it. Everything had been handed to him on a silver platter, and—infuriatingly—he thought he deserved it all. He thought it was his due.

She leaned back on the sofa, trying to make herself comfortable among the expanse of flowered chintz. She recalled her pride with embarrassment, or something else; but already she was planning. Her tidy mind told her that there was a quick, clean, and easy way out of this dilemma. She was sure that by thinking things through, quietly and clearly, she would find it. Then she would let the rest of the board members know how to proceed.

A mile and a half from Sandra Albee's house stood a small clapboard house, two stories high, surrounded by enormous yew hedges and a small garden. In spring, the garden gave birth to a fabulous array of azaleas, dogwood blossoms, irises, and daffodils, but now, two full weeks after the first killing frost of winter, the place had a degraded look. Without the flowers and greenery to brighten it, the house could be seen for what it was: a square little lump of a thing, without grace and without humor. Rather like its owner.

Leticia Sanderson didn't mind the look of her house. She felt inviolable; and it would be evident to any visitor (if there were any, which there weren't) that felicity and joy were frowned upon within the precincts of Leticia's abode. Leticia had taken the notion of by-the-book housekeeping to its logical conclusion, and beyond. The place had the rigidity of an army barracks, or a prison.

She herself was neat, to a degree that was off-putting. There had been a time, in her unambitious youth, when she had worn her hair long and had preferred flowering caftans to slacks or skirts. Today her wardrobe consisted mainly of khaki skirts of varying weights, or (in winter) khaki trousers; the skirts or slacks were almost invariably paired with navy blue blazers and oxford-cloth shirts.

On this, the first Saturday of the winter vacation, Leticia was heavily occupied. She bristled and bustled as she sat at a small Formica-topped desk in her library, a neat stack of index cards before her. The task ahead wouldn't be easy.

She had realized on Friday, as soon as Salgo's

departure had been announced, that she had to make the most of the brief winter holiday. She knew that her title of Acting Head was just temporary—there had been a hole to plug, and the board had plugged it with her. She might even be replaced before the start of the next term. Leticia Sanderson was nobody's fool, and she didn't for a minute think that she could stay on as head without some heavy spadework. Otherwise, she knew she didn't stand a chance.

This morning, ballpoint pen in hand, she had carefully read the latest edition of the *Hamilton Quill*. Dependable little weekly that it was, it provided detailed news about a host of activities going on in town during this festive season—bazaars, concerts, bake sales, audiences with Santa, Hanukkah charity dinners, and pre-Christmas festivities of all sorts. Leticia had made a file card for every event, indicating on each card which of the eleven Jefferson board members were likely to turn up. Then she had made herself a rigorous schedule. With careful planning and excellent timing, she should manage to put herself in the way of seven board members before the week was through. She knew some of them fairly well—old Hamiltonians, like Susan Miles, who had been one of the first people Leticia met when she came to town, and Tony Zimmerman, a prominent local attorney, who had dated her briefly a dozen or so years ago—well, once, if she were being honest.

These people would be easy enough to work on; she had good relations with most of them. George Farnham she wasn't sure of; but he would definitely be on hand for the Hamilton Free Library's annual reading of *A Christmas Carol*, which was scheduled for Monday afternoon. He always read the part of Marley's ghost. She put a faint check mark beside George's name.

She reviewed the cards. There were a few trouble spots—one in particular. She would never get the nod from the board if that Albee woman was permitted to vote.

Leticia detested Sandra Albee, with her odious little salmon-colored suits and her pearl necklaces and her endless ideas about running everyone else's life. So, that was one thing. Somehow, Albee would have to be knocked off the board, or at least taken temporarily out of play. Once Leticia had the job, she could win Albee over with some trifling nod to the woman's superior economic status, or by inviting her to serve on some kind of organizing committee. Albee adored committees, and always seemed to have time to serve whenever invited. It would just be a matter of time. But Leticia now regretted the snubs she had administered in the past. Oh well, bygones were bygones.

The jangle of the telephone shattered her reverie. Reluctantly, she reached for the receiver.

"Hello?"

"Leticia, hi. It's Jennifer Hatch."

Leticia groaned inwardly. The head of the Parent-Teacher Community Coordinating Committee, Jennifer Hatch was one person who knew how to be a pain in the neck. Ordinarily, Leticia would have cut her off in short order; but it was time to play politics. Leticia Sanderson might not have a master's degree, but she had certainly done advanced studies in politics.

"It's been a long time," she said, trying to sound chatty and upbeat. "I'm glad you called— I was on the point of picking up the phone to call you. How are you?"

"Fine. Listen, I'm sorry to disturb you on your first day of vacation, if you can call it that. But there are some important issues that the committee feels need to be addressed, and perhaps I should wait until after vacation, but I don't see what difference that makes, really. So I hope you'll be willing to hear me out."

"Jennifer, you know that we always welcome feedback from our parents. You're not disturbing me in the least." Leticia waited, expecting the worst. She got it.

Jennifer Hatch launched into an obviously prepared speech, full of admonishments about the difficulties of Leticia's job as Acting Head. Barely disguised was an attitude of condescension mixed with apprehension, as though Leticia didn't have an ounce of sense, nor a clue about the Jefferson and its reputation, its traditions. As if she were some last-choice babysitter, come to watch over a precious child whose regular nanny was out of commission. A bench-warmer, a water-boy, allowed to play in the big game through circumstances beyond everyone's control.

Leticia played the role that, in her years as Supervisor for Student Affairs, she had come to detest. She talked smoothly and fluently, keeping herself in the background and the school in the foreground. When it suited her, Leticia could be quite charming, and it suited her now. Jennifer Hatch, placated somewhat by Leticia's reassuring words, unbent a little, ending the call on a more cooperative note.

When she hung up the phone, Leticia was more determined than ever. She was sick of soothing egos, sick of being passed over, sick to death of everything and everybody that stood in her way. Salgo was out. Soon, Albee would be off the board. That would only leave Rigton Blair to work on.

She drew a fresh file card from the pack and picked up her fountain pen. RIGTON BLAIR, she wrote in large black letters. STRATEGY.

Then she sat back, lost in thought.

Feeling somewhat out of his depth, Murray Hill pulled his Volkswagen Beetle up in front of Victor Salgo's house. He studied the windows—which were uncurtained, giving the place an unlived-in look, but then Salgo was a single man, like himself, and probably had little interest in decorating. Any touches of grace inside or out were probably the work of the Hamilton Garden Club or the Parent-Teacher Community Coordinating Committee, who saw to it that the headmaster had a decently furnished living room and a suitably book-lined den.

Salgo's silver BMW was parked in the driveway; its owner was sure to be home. But when Hill pulled open the storm door, he nearly tripped over the uncollected mail at his feet, including a small package. Curious, he picked it up and studied the handwriting: feminine, with lots of flourishes, immature; it reminded Hill of the writing of the girls in his tenth-grade English class. As a schoolteacher he came across this kind of writing every day, but it surprised him to see it on a package, here on Salgo's doorstep. The postmark was blurred, and there was no return address.

He leaned down and picked up the other pieces of mail—a few bills, three catalogs (one, he noted without humor, from Victoria's Secret) and the everyday range of junk mail. Nothing personal except for the package.

Fairly certain that Salgo wouldn't answer, Hill rang the bell anyway and dutifully waited. He rang again. Then, glad for the momentary reprieve, he put the mail back on the doorsill, shut the storm door carefully, and bundled himself

back into his car. He would have to try again, he
knew—but maybe, despite the presence of the
BMW, Salgo *had* gone off to Reno or somewhere, by air or on the train. Maybe Hill could
let the matter rest until the end of vacation.

He headed for home.

6

THE HAMILTON FREE Library was usually closed on Sundays, but on this day Dewey and her cast were rehearsing for their annual reading of *A Christmas Carol*, scheduled for the next evening. (Admission, three dollars: proceeds to the Hamilton Library.)

Dewey had rigged up a modest set on the raised platform of the Children's Reading Room, and she was busily adjusting chairs and stools for the cast members. The part of Scrooge was taken, as always by Fielding Booker, Hamilton's captain of police. He was the only twentieth-century man Dewey knew who looked perfectly natural in a nightcap—but then he really wasn't wholly a twentieth-century man. Even on ordinary occasions he had about him an air of belonging to the past, an aura that was heightened by his formal good manners and old-fashioned suits and hats and walking sticks. The part of the beleaguered Bob Cratchit would be read by Murray Hill, who Dewey always thought of as "that nice young man from the Jeff"—although Dewey had known him for ten years, and he wasn't as young as he once had been. Dewey's colleague, Tom Campbell, would be the Ghost of Christmas Past; he considered his roundly oratorical, pompous voice as perfectly suited to the part, and Dewey wasn't about to contradict him. Nils Reichart, publican, would serve as the narrator, and various children of the town had been chosen to portray the burgeoning Cratchit family. After the reading, the Wolf Tones would sing a few Christmas carols, and punch would be served.

With the exception of the children, the cast all knew their parts nearly by heart—the result of years of repetition. The reading was always a popular event in Hamilton; Dewey sometimes thought it was simply the promise of seeing Fielding Booker in a nightshirt that drew them back year after year. Today she noted with pleasure that everything was going unusually smoothly. Even Tom Campbell, who constantly lost his place and had to be clued in by Dewey from her prompter's spot behind the Teen Mystery section, was getting into the swing of things. If only he wouldn't try to affect a British accent, Dewey thought, he might not be half bad.

When Tiny Tim had uttered his "God bless us, every one," and Dewey had spoken a few words of instruction regarding the performance, the cast began to scatter.

"Um, Mrs. James?" said a small voice. Dewey looked down; it was Tommy Reynolds, who was playing the part of Tiny Tim. Eight years old, with blond hair and big brown eyes, Tommy could look waiflike and angelic if he chose. Dewey knew he was neither.

"Tommy, you were wonderful," she said brightly. "Were you nervous?"

"Nah."

"I didn't think so. All ready for tomorrow's big performance?"

"Yup." He shifted from one foot to another, glancing around apprehensively. "Um, Mrs. James?"

Tommy was not ordinarily given to standing around talking to old ladies. By now it was clear to Dewey that he had something on his mind. "Is there anything I can help you with?" she asked, leading him out of the Children's Reading Room and down a short hallway that led to her office. Maybe he wanted a quiet place to talk. Or maybe the problem would be solved when they reached the door marked Gentlemen.

Suddenly Tommy stopped and looked grave. "Can you do me a favor?"

"What's that?"

"Well, I'm kind of in trouble."

"Oh, dear." Dewey couldn't imagine this boy in serious trouble. He was a good child, honest and generous.

"See, I sort of disobeyed my mom."

"Aha." Well, that kind of trouble was usually easily mended, thought Dewey. She was still in the dark about how she might come into it. "And?"

"She thinks that the Goose Bumps are too scary for me, and she told me 'no more.'"

"Ah," said Dewey, understanding all. The Goose Bumps were a series of short novels—tales of terror, involving mummies and monsters of all types—wildly popular with young males eight to eleven. Tommy, Dewey knew, had read them all, some of them more than once, and he apparently raised his threshold for terror with each succeeding story. Last week, she had turned down his request to take out a collection of stories by H.P. Lovecraft. Those, she believed, really might frighten him. But the Goose Bumps were harmless enough, although not to her taste. "When did the edict go into effect?"

"Huh?"

"When did your mother tell you no more Goose Bumps?"

"A while ago," mumbled Tommy.

"Last week? Last month?"

"Um, like maybe in September."

Oh, dear, thought Dewey. She had been happily serving up contraband to this young man for three full months. Margaret Reynolds would have to be told the truth. Dewey folded her arms and looked sternly at the boy. "You shouldn't have tricked me, Tommy."

"I know." Tommy hung his head, a sure sign that he wasn't really sorry. He looked up suddenly at Dewey. Though he was doing his best to look contrite, his eyes were bright with mischief. "Do you think we could just make a deal?"

"What kind of deal?" Dewey felt herself softening.

"I mean, Mom's so dumb anyway. It's not like I really believe in all that stuff. It doesn't scare me."

"Maybe it scares *her*."

"Nah. But she thinks I believe it."

Dewey sighed. Margaret Reynolds was a little overprotective, but not the type to worry about Tommy's reading habits; there must have been some sort of Incident. Dewey opened the door to her office, motioned Tommy to a chair, and seated herself behind the desk. "Tell me the story from the beginning," she said. "Then we shall see what can be done."

"Well, see, the problem is that Mom didn't believe me the other day when I told her about something." Tommy halted, uncertain. "Something I saw."

"What did you see?"

"Well, it looked like a ghost."

"Do you believe in ghosts?"

"Nope. I only said it *looked* like one, not that it *was* one." Tommy was suddenly scornful. Grown-ups. Even when you thought you could count on them, they could be so dumb.

"All right, then, what was it?"

"I don't know. See, my binoculars don't work too well at night—my dad says because they're not wide enough, and his telescope is downstairs and I didn't want to make any noise."

From this, Dewey understood that the ghost had appeared outdoors, some distance away, during the night. The Reynoldses lived on top of a big hill, not far from Dewey. Their house was surrounded on three sides by forest, and the property backed up to the Boone River, up above the dam. There wasn't much of a prospect, because the woods were so dark. The only vista would be straight ahead, down the long road that led into town. "So you had to use your binoculars," prompted Dewey, interested. "Where was the—the, er, thing?"

"Across the river."

"Through the woods?"

"Well, you can really see into the woods now because two big trees came down in last year's storm. So you can see pretty far, if you know just how to look."

Which undoubtedly Tommy did know. "What were you looking for?"

"I wanted to know about the light."

"You saw a light shining in the woods."

"Through the woods. Up on the other side of Johnson's Ravine."

"Ah." Dewey thought quickly. There wasn't much up on the other side of the river there—just the back end of old Route 52, which led in one direction to the dump and in the other back to Cutter's Lane, which would take you back to town. A light there would naturally pique the interest of a boy like Tommy. "You saw a light, you got out your binoculars, and you saw something that looked like a ghost."

"Yeah. Well, it looked like somebody in a sheet for Halloween, if you know what I mean."

"Perfectly." Dewey nodded. "Were you frightened?"

"'Course not. Anyway, it went away."

"Into the woods?"

"Up the hill."

"How very odd," remarked Dewey, more to herself than to the boy. "What time was this, Tommy?"

Tommy shrugged. "Maybe around one or two. I didn't check. But I was asleep and I woke up."

"And you told your parents."

Tommy took a deep breath. Evidently they had arrived at the crucial point. The boy hurried through a little speech. "My mom asked me why I was so tired and I told her, and she got all mad and said I was reading with my flashlight, but I wasn't, I was looking out the window, and then she went into my room and she found my book and my flashlight hidden under my pillow and she got *really* mad." He took another deep breath. "And," he finished up, "I think she's kind of mad at you too, Mrs. James, because you weren't supposed to give me any more Goose Bumps."

"Don't worry about that; I'm sure she'll accept your explanation and your apology." Dewey smiled. "And how about if you let me give you something else to read?" They made their way back to the children's section, and Dewey selected an old Hardy Boys for Tommy: *The Hidden Harbor Mystery*. She checked the book out for him at the front desk. "It's old-fashioned, but I think you'll like it."

"Okay." Tommy grinned. "Thanks, Mrs. James. Sorry if I got you in trouble."

"I'll get over it, Tommy." Dewey ruffled his hair. "But no more Goose Bumps for a while."

"I've read 'em all. And anyway, my friend Bobby's got some books by Stephen King." He gave Dewey an impertinent little smile and waved happily as he headed out into the cold December air.

After the rehearsal George Farnham had given Dewey a quick nod and slipped out the front door, catching up with Murray Hill on the library steps.

"Got a minute?"

"Sure, George." Hill was not at all surprised to be accosted this way. He knew that there had been an emergency meeting of the school board that morning. Presumably Rigton Blair had spoken to them about Hill's mission. "It's about Salgo?"

"Yes and no. How about a coffee?"

"All right." The two men walked briskly up Slingluff Street, the wind biting through their overcoats; in less than five minutes they had secured themselves a quiet booth in the back of Josie's Place, one of Hamilton's finest traditional establishments. Over coffee and chess pie they talked about the situation.

"I know that Blair approached you," said Farnham. "He wanted me to take it on, but I thought the business of getting Salgo to sign would be better dealt with through less formal channels. I'm sorry if I've made your vacation burdensome."

"Not at all." Murray Hill waved away George's apology. "I'm sure everything will be fine. The only thing is, I've got to find Salgo."

"Isn't he around?"

"Who knows? I went by the house yesterday afternoon, and again today on my way to rehearsal. He'll turn up."

"Did you call him first?"

"Nope." Hill shook his head. "The truth is, I

thought it would be easier to get it over with if I just kind of dropped by."

George gave Hill a thoughtful look. "In other words, you didn't want to give him the time to think about it."

"You could put it like that."

"Well, I wouldn't think there's any need to hurry. In spite of Rigton Blair's worries, I'm convinced that Salgo has no intention of turning up in January to demand his old job back."

"No, you're probably right. I think he was getting ready to pack it in anyway."

"What makes you say that?"

"Oh, just the way he was about everything. Look, we weren't in the same department, but I got to know him a bit while he was teaching math. He was pretty good in the classroom, and it was obvious that the stuff came naturally to him. I heard he was some kind of statistical whiz kid in college, and he probably should have been on Wall Street—but I guess he got stuck. Professionally."

George nodded. He had seen that sort of thing happen over and over. "Did he mention changing careers?"

Murray Hill shook his head. "No, but he talked a lot about getting rich."

"Maybe that amounted to the same thing," commented George.

"Well, he has a head for math. But he doesn't like people much."

"Not a great character trait for a headmaster."

"Right. I mean, the job is only half academic administration; the rest of it is community relations, dealing with the parents, keeping up the spirits of the faculty. It's not a job for someone who doesn't understand people."

George Farnham took a moment to reflect. He didn't really know Salgo, except to nod to him here at Josie's Place, or in the hardware store on a Saturday morning. But what little he had seen of the man hadn't impressed him. He had always wondered how the trustees had chosen him, and finally assumed that Salgo had some sort of appeal that wasn't immediately obvious. Now it looked as though there hadn't been anything to recommend him after all. Why on earth *had* the trustees chosen him in the first place?

"Murray, I want to ask you something in confidence, seeing that I have suddenly been pressed into service for the Jeff. I wasn't a member of the board last year when Salgo was appointed, nor am I a full-term member now. I'm only there temporarily, but unfortunately my tenure coincides with this emergency. I'd like to be more in the picture. If what you say is true, what's the scuttlebutt? Why was Victor Salgo given the job to begin with? I know you can't speak for the board. But tell me the faculty viewpoint."

Hill looked uncomfortable. "I don't know, George. Schools are full of rumor and innuendo. They're breeding grounds for all kinds of gossip. I try to keep out of it."

"Very commendable, Murray. But you must have an opinion. What do you think?"

"All right. I think he was definitely the wrong guy for the job—the point's academic now, of course, since he no longer has the job. But, that said, I think that maybe there were some people who figured the Jeff's profile had become a little—well, let's call it one-dimensional. You familiar with the term 'white bread'?"

"Hmm," said Farnham. "You don't mean the stuff for sandwiches. The Jeff is too WASPy?"

"You could put it that way. So, maybe the board thought that by making Salgo headmaster they could balance things."

"Along ethnic lines."

"That's right." Hill laughed. "The joke was on the board. According to Vivian the Vivacious—"

"Who?"

"The administration's head secretary. She knows everything."

"Ah, yes. Vivian Freshet." George conjured up an image of her: neat, always impeccably turned out, with glossy jet-black hair falling neatly to her collar. "Yes, she would know everything. What did she tell you?"

"Just that the Board thought it was great that his name ended with an *o*."

"Aha."

"Apparently, Salgo thought it was hilarious."

"Why?"

Hill shrugged his shoulders. "Who knows?"

The two men sat in silence for a few moments, concentrating on Josie's chess pie (the best in the Boone Valley) and coffee (always a little too strong). Finally, Murray Hill spoke again.

"I'm going to pass by his house again on my way home. And I don't think I'm the only person looking for him."

"Oh? Why's that?"

"Because yesterday when I went by, there was a big pile of mail, kind of jammed in between the storm door and the front door. I nearly fell over it."

"Oh—well, maybe he's been home, took it in."

"No." Hill shook his head firmly. "No, the mail was still there today. But there's a package missing."

"Are you sure?"

"Positive." Hill described the little brown-paper-wrapped package with the childish handwriting. "It was there yesterday, and I noticed it because it looked as if it might have come from a student. You know, the way girls write. Dot their *i*'s with little hearts, make a squiggly line under words."

"And it wasn't there this morning?"

"Nope."

"Strange." George finished the last of his pie.

"But he'll be back, I'm sure. He loves that Beamer of his, and he won't let it just sit and rot in his driveway."

"He didn't put it in the garage?"

"Nope, it's just sitting there, as if he came home in a hurry."

"Well, maybe he took a plane somewhere." George glanced out the huge plate-glass window at the street outside. The wind was blowing, and fat drops of icy rain were beginning to fall. "Some sunny weather. Maybe he hopped it for Florida."

Murray Hill rolled his eyes. "What people see in Florida, George, is something I'll never understand. Give me a nice cold winter, any day." Hill rose to go. "Nice talking with you, George. See you tomorrow."

7

On Monday morning Dewey was pleasantly surprised to hear the roar of a motorcycle blasting its way up her driveway. She paused in her labors (trying to clean out the mysterious nether reaches of the refrigerator) to look out the window.

The roar stopped, and a tall, bespectacled, leather-suited man dismounted. Dewey hurriedly wiped her hands and went to open the kitchen door.

"Howdy, Dew," said the man, taking off his helmet and stooping slightly to kiss her cheek. "Hope you don't mind my dropping in unannounced."

"Why, Franklin. It's been an age!" Dewey replied cheerfully. It had been several months since she'd seen Franklin Lowe, but they had been good friends since childhood. Franklin had taught Latin and Greek at the Jefferson School for as long as Dewey could remember. He had never married; his fiancée had been killed in a train wreck in France when he was a young man, and most Hamiltonians felt he had never gotten over it. He had simply buried himself in his work, introducing generation after generation of Jefferson boys (and now girls too) to the rigors of the classical languages and the excitement of scholarship. Occasionally he emerged to socialize in town life, and he was well-liked wherever he went. He was an aficionado of bluegrass music, and he played a lightning banjo. Some people who didn't know him found him eccentric, but Dewey thought they were put off by the motorcycle. Franklin himself had always found it odd that more people didn't ride motorcycles.

He came in, looked around approvingly, put his helmet on the kitchen table, and pulled up a chair for himself. "How about some coffee for an old friend?" he said, unzipping his leather jacket and folding his tall frame storklike onto the small ladder-back wooden chair.

Dewey smiled and cheerfully obliged, chatting amiably about this and that—the Dickens reading scheduled for tonight in the library; her daughter, Grace, due home next week to spend Christmas; the garden; her mare, Starbuck. As he sipped his coffee, Franklin listened appreciatively, clearly taking pleasure in hearing Dewey talk.

Finally he broke into her stream of chatter. He leaned forward and clasped his hands on the table. "Listen, Dewey, I came here for a reason."

"You always have a reason, Franklin, although you certainly don't need one." She gave him a shrewd look.

"I ought to know better, Dewey, than never to come calling except when I need you."

She waved this concern away. "Don't be ridiculous. What can I do for you?"

"Here's the thing, Dewey. You know that Victor Salgo is no longer the head of the Jeff."

"Yes, Franklin. Of course I know. It's all anyone's talking about this week."

"Yes, I suppose so. Well, the thing is this. Nobody was particularly sorry to hear that he'd resigned. He just wasn't cut out for the job." Franklin laughed. "Boy, you should have seen the way some of the parents looked at him. Well, you know—they cut him dead, basically."

"I can imagine." Dewey visualized the soft, faintly pear-shaped Salgo, with his mustache and his slightly shiny suits. She could well imagine that some of the snobs in town might find him not-quite-the-thing, even were he dynamic and charming. Which he was not. "He must have found it hard."

"I don't think he even noticed, Dewey, which of course made it all the worse. He just isn't a very clued-in type of fellow. One-track mind, really."

"How on earth did he get the job, Franklin?"

He waved a hand. "Oh, it was one of those silly attempts to make up for things. Even though he opposed Salgo's appointment, Rigton Blair, that monumental horse's posterior, thought that having an Hispanic headmaster would make the Jeff more culturally diverse." Franklin laughed. "The joke being, of course, that Salgo isn't Hispanic at all."

"No?" Dewey smiled.

"No—Montenegrin, I think, or something like that. He's a little mysterious about it, probably because he likes to have the laugh on Blair."

"Not a very mature way of dealing with things," noted Dewey.

"Well, that's right. Maturity isn't his long suit. Anyway, the Salgo chapter is closed, thank the Lord, although regrettably we now face another challenge."

"Leticia Sanderson," said Dewey.

Franklin nodded. "One and the same. I am petitioning the gods, Dewey, and seeing auguries everywhere. I hope we can count on the board this time around. The faculty are conducting an anonymous survey, just in case anyone ever asks for our opinion. Which, of course, they won't."

"Don't be too sure," said Dewey. "George

Farnham is on the board now, you know. He's a man of sense."

"Yes, but what can one man do?" Lowe grinned. "He's up against that awful Albee woman, who just likes to get her own way for the sake of it, and Blair, and a carload of up-and-coming corporation vice-presidents. Not exactly an easy bunch to overpower, our board."

"Maybe that will change."

"Maybe not."

"Well, why would Leticia Sanderson get the job, anyway, Franklin? She's not qualified. I think she barely managed to get her high school diploma—and what I could tell you about her reading habits would shock you."

"Hah. Nothing you could tell me about that woman would shock me." Franklin let out a sigh. "But who knows? More multiculturalism? Time for a woman head? The times conspire against us, Dewey. But like any institution, the Jeff can only be as good as its head. And the Jeff, I'm afraid, is about to be a thing of the past."

"What on earth do you mean?"

"I mean this: The school is headed for trouble, Dewey. There is something missing, shifting, changing—being lost. Call it standards, perhaps. Salgo knew, I think, that he was the emblem of the coming mediocrity. Not because he wasn't WASPy, but because he wasn't any good. Didn't care."

"I'm sure you're just fantasizing, Franklin. It's easy to slip into—I do it myself all the time."

Lowe shook his head. "I wish that were the case, Dewey. But there's been something—something leaving the Jeff, lately. Since before Salgo took over, even, although it's been more noticeable over the last few years."

Now Dewey was getting impatient. "But I still don't know what you mean. Something missing how? In terms of the way the school is run?"

"I mean academically."

"Oh, well—"

Lowe held up a hand. "Hear me out. It's a subjective thing, you know, but it bears thinking about. I know when students are meeting a certain academic standard; and in its hundred-year history, the Jeff has consistently maintained a very high level of academic performance. Over the last few years I have seen these standards slip. In my classroom, and in other areas around the school."

"Maybe you're just expecting too much, Franklin. Last I heard, the graduating seniors were all bound for excellent colleges, with half of them taking advanced placement in three or four subjects."

Franklin smiled. "The world isn't what it used to be, is it, Dewey?" He sipped the last of his coffee. "Anyway, I didn't come here to moan and groan about the disappearance of standards in academia. In fact, I came here to enlist your help in solving a little mystery."

"Ooh," said Dewey. She was famous in Hamilton—and in other places around the globe—for loving to solve little mysteries. Sometimes they turned out to be quite big mysteries. "What's it about?"

"About Victor Salgo. He seems to have disappeared."

Dewey, disappointed, waved the mystery away. "I'm sure he's gone off for a little vacation. If I were in his shoes, I'd clear out of Hamilton pretty quick."

"I agree—but listen. Last Thursday—which by coincidence, or maybe not, was Salgo's last day at the school—he stopped by my office. We talked of this and that for five minutes, and then he asked me to let him borrow my guitar. He was supposed to play in the Winter Pageant, and he hadn't practiced, and his own guitar was in the shop or something."

"I didn't know he played," remarked Dewey.

"Oh, yes. He's not bad, actually. Well, you can imagine that I wasn't in a position to say no to the headmaster, especially since he had me on the spot. If I'd had time to think about it, I would have found a diplomatic way to refuse. But there we were in my office, and the guitar was right there, and I had to say yes."

"I suppose you did," agreed Dewey.

Lowe shook his head. "Well, you know what

happened. Suddenly Salgo resigned, and he didn't even turn up at school on Friday to address the students and faculty. He just vanished, and my Ovation with him."

"Isn't that a little strong?" asked Dewey. "Surely if you call him—"

Lowe shook his head. "I've tried calling, and I've tried stopping by. His car is there, that flashy silver thing, but he isn't at home. At a guess, I'd say he hasn't been home since last Friday. There are newspapers, mail, all sorts of things piled up inside the storm door."

"Perhaps he's feeling awkward," offered Dewey.

"Frankly, I don't care about his feelings, I want my guitar back." He flashed Dewey a grin. "And you're just the person to recover it for me."

"How so?"

Lowe counted off the reasons on his fingers. "One: You have no qualms about inserting yourself delicately into the lives of others. Two: You're my friend and you know how important my guitar is to me. And three: You're just as curious as I am, now, about the strange behavior and untimely disappearance of Mr. Victor Salgo."

8

THE LITTLE LIBRARY was packed to overflowing by five-thirty that afternoon. Outside, a gentle snowfall had begun, and the stragglers coming in the door were wiping the snowflakes from their hair as they stamped their feet. Within, the little stage in the Children's Reading Room had been decked out with the same props Dewey had used in years past—a painted, Victorian-looking window giving onto a wintry London street scene; a high, backless stool and tall table for poor overworked Bob Cratchit, a bedpost (just one) to represent Ebenezer Scrooge's bedroom. From behind a nearby row of shelves, the voices of children could be heard, practicing their parts. Over in the Reference section the adults were being expertly made up by Doris Bock, proprietor of the Tidal Wave Beauty Salon. Little Mary Barstow, dental hygienist, was relishing her role as costume mistress; her duties (at this moment) required her to assist Murray Hill, who was struggling with an old-fashioned high, stiff collar. Mary's dexterous little fingers worked nimbly, adjusting the collar and cravat and smoothing down the front of Hill's shirt. She ran a hand over his hair and smiled coyly. "Are you as old-fashioned as you look?" she asked him.

"Lamentably so, ma'am," replied Hill, the shadow of an apologetic smile playing across his handsome features, "bein' Dixie born and bred. I thank you for your kind assistance." He returned her hands gently to where they belonged. She smiled again, but by now had shifted her attention elsewhere. She hastily finished with Hill and trained her sights on Tom Campbell, who was struggling into an odd assortment of vaguely old-fashioned, thoroughly moth-eaten clothes. "Can I help you with the buttons?" she called out cheerfully. Tom Campbell, ever preserving his dignity, nodded his assent, and Mary's nimble little fingers found another practice area. With such sublime motor skills, she was an excellent dental hygienist.

Dewey, taking tickets at the front desk, was pleased with the turnout. This little ritual had begun nearly thirty years ago as Dewey's brainchild—in those days she had earmarked the revenues from ticket sales for the purchase of books by and about Charles Dickens. As the years wore on, the Dickens section was filled, and the money was used to buy books by various other Victorian authors and on related subjects. Today the Hamilton Free Library has one of the country's finest collections of literary Victoriana—but the annual readings of *A Christmas Carol* continue. Dewey and Tom Campbell had gotten permission from the Town Council to spend this year's ticket revenues on some fancy new computer software; Tom, with a rare glint of humor, told the council members that the old program "originally belonged to Philip Marley, who left it to the library in his will."

There will be no surprises in the performance; everyone in the audience knows exactly what to expect, but still they always come back. The actors took their places on tall stools around the stage, with their parts before them in large, elegant construction-paper binders (made by the fourth-grade class at the Jefferson School). The lights went down, and bearded, burly, bass-toned Nils Reichart began to read. The audience quieted, listening raptly to the tale. Dewey loved this story and never tired of it; it seemed to her that there was much to be learned from it, year after year.

When Marley's ghost (George Farnham) made its clanking appearance, dragging the chain forged in life, the audience was utterly silent. Dewey, happening to glance toward Tommy

Reynolds, noted that the boy looked nervous. She doubted it was stage fright; perhaps his mother was right, and the Goose Bumps were too scary. She scanned the audience until she spotted Margaret Reynolds. Dewey knew the woman well, and had always found her to be very reasonable with Tommy in the matter of reading material—unlike some mothers, who were forever censoring what their children read. There was little you could do with such people, except hope that their offspring wouldn't cease to be inquisitive in the face of deadening restrictions on their intellectual curiosity. But Margaret Reynolds was different, not like that. If the Goose Bumps were out of bounds, there was probably a respectable reason for it. Dewey resolved to talk to her that afternoon, after the performance. For now, she turned her attention back to the little stage, where a trembling Fielding Booker was beholding the Christmases of his past.

In the third row from the back, Leticia Sanderson, looking anything but Christmasy in her standard khaki skirt, blue blazer, and oxford-cloth shirt, sat clutching a small stack of index cards. Every now and then she glanced down at them; her notes were written in code—letters, followed by names and handwritten symbols. She was hoping to knock off about ten prospective votes here at this idiot ritual. Ordinarily,

Leticia wouldn't be caught dead listening to her fellow Hamiltonians make fools of themselves. The only decent performance, for her money, was being turned in by Tom Campbell. But he was a very erudite man, and he had a nice, quasi-British accent. Leticia wondered idly where he'd learned to speak so well.

She turned her attention back to her notes. Today, at the punch-party following the performance, she should be able to buttonhole George Farnham, Tony Zimmerman, and possibly even Susan Miles, who was playing Scrooge's niece. She looked up from her cards and noted that George seemed, unfortunately, to be on very friendly terms with that drip Murray Hill. Thought he was God's gift to education, that little twit. Well, Leticia would see to it that he got his comeuppance—as soon as she got permanent approval by the board. For now, she would let it slide. He might as well finish out the year.

Leticia was also bothered by the presence of Franklin Lowe in the audience. Two faculty members—well, she probably should have expected it. There might even be more. She would have to see to it that they didn't get between her and her objectives. She looked once more at her cards: Susan Miles (according to Leticia's strategy) could be had by assuring places for her two daughters at the Jeff. Tony Zimmerman was a horse breeder as well as a noted attorney;

Leticia was all ready to talk to him about the prospect of initiating a broad-based equestrian program at the school. She had heard that Tony's income was on the low side for a lawyer— probably because he did a lot of sappy *pro bono* work, she reasoned. To ease his conscience, maybe, over being a horse breeder in the first place.

She paused in her reflections to marvel once more at how easy it was to manipulate most people. Everybody was the same, really. Everyone needed to be flattered, and most people—if you bothered to pay them a compliment—were vain enough to think that what you said was true. Leticia didn't even do it consciously, really; it was something that just came naturally to her. These days.

She smiled to herself, a quick, sad little smile, and went back to her index cards, her face a mask.

Leticia's childhood friends could have told you that even as a young girl she had been acutely aware of the sensitive spots of others— the things they disliked about themselves, their undisclosed sources of pain, their secret longings. She knew just how to apply a salve—of comfort, of hope—which nearly always made people grateful. And grateful people are generally useful to their benefactors.

Leticia's grownup acquaintances could tell you that the secret of her adult success was

neither empathy nor solace, although her in-
sights often masqueraded as such. But Leticia
was neither kind nor compassionate. She was, at
heart, an utter stranger to human affinity and
fellow feeling; her kindness gained her leverage,
and her proffered balm was often a scourge.

"How many people did we have, Dewey?"
asked George Farnham. They were dining in his
riverfront house, more specifically in the enormous kitchen in which he spent most of his
waking hours. George was an excellent cook,
and over the last few years—as he and Dewey
had made dining together at his place more and
more of a ritual—he had expanded his kitchen
repertoire impressively. The oversized industrial
stove, the large, gleaming copper pots, and the
fancy electrical gadgets and whirlers and gizmos
that lined the long countertop all saw plenty of
use.

George's kitchen also had a big fieldstone
fireplace and sliding glass doors that opened
onto a porch and the river. In summer, Dewey
and George loved to sit on the porch, drink a
cocktail, and listen to the rushing water; in
winter, Dewey found herself more and more at
home next to George's fireplace, with birch logs
sparking and a glass of good red wine.

George had built the kitchen himself—the
house was an old textile factory that he had
converted, after his wife's death, into a palatial

widower's residence. It was utterly unlike his old farmhouse, which had been, like Dewey's, cozy and countrified. George had needed a drastic change to cope with losing Lois. In his ultra-modern, loftlike house, he had found the comfort that had eluded him in softer surroundings.

Tonight, he and Dewey were going over the exciting events of the afternoon. George's face still bore traces of pancake makeup and eyeliner—Mary Barstow had been eager to help him take it off, but he had fled her cold cream and her ministrations for the privacy of his own bathroom, and the pleasure of an evening with Dewey James. Now they were dining on a simple lamb cassoulet, accompanied by freshly baked French bread and a bottle of Merlot. Outside, the gentle snowfall continued; the flakes were white flutters in the air as they passed through the outside light on George's porch.

"There were a hundred and twenty-three people, George, if you can believe it. We made almost four hundred dollars, which is *ample* for that new whatsit that Tom Campbell wants."

"Software."

"Yes, as I said." Dewey's blue eyes twinkled. She liked to play the role of old-fashioned computer ignoramus, but in fact she understood their library's little system far better than her younger colleague. Her secret was not believing too much in the thing. She had steadfastly refused to throw away the old card catalog, and now it sat in her own attic. One day, she knew, history would thank her for preserving a slice of representative twentieth-century scholarship.

"Well, anyway, my dear. I congratulate you. How many years does this make it?"

"Thirty-seven, I think, George. But who's counting? All I know is that Tommy Reynolds' father played Tiny Tim in our original production."

"Nice boy, Tommy," commented George.

"He *is* nice. George, do you know that the other day he took me aside to apologize for getting me in trouble with his mother?" She told George the story of the Goose Bumps books. "He was feeling rather guilty, I think."

George chuckled. "Hoodwinked you, did he? Was Margaret angry with you?"

"Not at all. I had a chance to talk to her tonight, after the reading, and she laughed about it. There's really no harm in the books, although I can't say I'd want to read them myself. They're all full of ghosts and mummies and vampires and all those dreadful things."

"Never cared for the stuff, myself," admitted George. "But I don't really know what you can do about Tommy's tastes. It's good that he wants to read at all, instead of sitting glued to those idiot video games."

"I know. Well, at least for now Tommy seems happy—he's read all the Goose Bumps anyway, and now he's started on the Hardy Boys. The old ones, which seem a little dull and old-fashioned to me, but at least there aren't any vampires, and he's sure to increase his vocabulary of obsolescent words."

"What does he think of the lads from Bayport?" George's own sons had owned the entire collection of Hardy Boys stories, and George had read quite a few of them himself.

"He told me he wants to be a detective. Speaking of which, George—" and Dewey gave him an account of Franklin Lowe's visit.

"I don't see why he had to bother you about it," said George stiffly, when she was through.

"Why ever not, George?"

"Well, why should he? It's his guitar. He was foolish to lend it in the first place." George was suddenly, decidedly, out of sorts.

Dewey got up and cleared the dinner dishes, puzzling over George's sudden ill humor. "Do you think it intrusive of me to make a phone call? I think Franklin feels a bit awkward about hunting down Salgo, who until last week was his boss, and is now in disgrace. I think he's being tactful, that's all."

"There's no need to be tactful. Victor Salgo went to Florida."

"Oh. Well, I'll tell Franklin. Is that what he told the Jefferson board? When will he be back?"

George, on the point of saying that he didn't

know, realized that he couldn't treat Dewey so. He told her, in turn, all about his conversation with Murray Hill, and the board's concern that Salgo might turn up from his jaunt asking for his old job back.

"Now, who put that idea into everyone's head?" asked Dewey. "If he wanted to keep his job, all he had to do was nothing—he could still have gone off to Florida. It is vacation time, after all."

"I imagine the idea originated with Rigton Blair. In a sense, you can't blame him."

"Oh, I think I could always blame him for something. He is the most stuck-up, dried-up, self-satisfied old fig that there ever was."

"Now, Dewey, be nice," George chided.

"Why on earth be nice about Rigton Blair? He's never nice to anyone else. Come off it, George—you dislike him as much as I do."

"So I do," conceded George, chuckling. "So I do."

"The fact is," said Dewey, "Rigton Blair hates Salgo for being Hispanic, which he's not, and therefore wants to make sure that the man has burned all his bridges and can never reappear at the Jeff."

"Whoa, Dewey dear. I lost you there for a minute. He's not Hispanic?"

"No. He's Montenegrin—like Nero Wolfe."

"Ah."

"But he doesn't have that gentleman's brains,

unfortunately, or he never would have gotten himself into such a situation. George, you must help me find out when he's coming back from Florida, if that's where he went, so that I can get Franklin's guitar back to him."

George scowled but refrained from comment, merely leaning over to plant a kiss on Dewey's cheek. She smiled at him, and went right on talking.

9

It was Tommy Reynolds' great luck that today of all days there should be a fresh coating of snow on the ground. He loved to be the first to make tracks in fresh snow, although he didn't mind sharing that glory with the deer and raccoons and quail who inhabited the woods behind the house. Now that the deer-hunting season had closed, he was permitted to go out by himself in the morning, although his mother still insisted that he wear a bright orange safety vest. There were people who didn't respect the calendar, and Tommy had to admit it made him nervous. But these are the chances you have to take, he told himself, if you're going to be a great detective. Besides, on a Tuesday morning there wouldn't be very many hunters around. Most of them worked.

He took with him his binoculars, his pocket

knife (with magnifying glass) and several small plastic bags for collecting evidence. He had washed out the bags in hot water before leaving the house, so they would be sterile, because he knew (from watching the news on TV) that evidence could be contaminated. He also brought a flashlight, although it was a sunny day. The woods were full of little nooks and crannies where the sunlight didn't really penetrate.

It was a long way to his destination—he had to walk almost a mile downriver before getting to the rickety old bridge that went over to Cutter's Lane, and then it was a mile back up. But he was happy. He had a plan.

The truth was that Tommy was still just a little bit angry with his mother over the "ghost" incident. Tommy was a very rational, if adventurous, boy, and he didn't really like the way his mother had pooh-poohed his assertions. Of course he knew it wasn't a ghost, but he knew it was *something*. His mother thought it was just a nightmare, and he resented that. But he knew, now, what a good detective would do in the circumstances: investigate, and come home with hard evidence that could not be challenged.

He wasn't prepared for how difficult the descent would be into Johnson's Ravine. Sliding precariously, grabbing out for trees, he had a hard time of it, and it was difficult, from this angle, to judge exactly where the light had been.

The hillside here was very steep, and there was a broad swath that had been burned over a few years ago; the growth that had since sprung up was mostly wild grasses and pine seedlings. Down below, the Boone River was rushing at a fast pace; to Tommy's practiced ear, it sounded like the river was very high, although he couldn't really risk trying to see all the way down. He was afraid he might slip.

He looked through his binoculars toward his bedroom window every five feet or so, and after about twenty minutes of maneuvering he believed he had found the spot. Hot and sweaty, in spite of the cold, he sat down on a moss-covered rock and looked around.

There was a blanket of snow in the burned-over area, but very little here under the trees. Obviously, the person who had been walking with the light had stayed in the woods for cover—or maybe because the grassy part was too slippery. It might have been a smuggler, thought Tommy reasonably, rather than a burglar, because there wasn't very much out here that anybody would want to steal. In *The Secret of the Caves*, which he had started on last night, Frank and Joe were confronting a gang of smugglers. Tommy paused briefly in his meditations on crime to envy those boys such a wonderful father. Not that he would ever want anyone to replace his own dad, but it would have been nice if his father were a detective.

Then he'd have a fingerprint kit right at home, and probably a whole laboratory set up in the basement, and his father's friends on the police force would track license-plate numbers for him.

"License plate," said Tommy aloud. Something twigged at his mind—something he'd seen on his way down the hill. But it wasn't here, it was twenty yards away, in the grassy part, mostly covered by snow. He had been so intent on his descent that it hadn't really registered—he suddenly realized that a great detective has to be thinking all the time. He might have missed it—but that's what he had seen. The top edge of a license plate, blue with white letters. Slipping and sliding, grasping at seedlings, he made his way to where he thought it lay. It took some careful doing, but in the end he got it.

Connecticut. Somebody had thrown away a Connecticut license plate in Johnson's Ravine.

Or had it been thrown away? To Tommy's admittedly inexpert eye, it looked as if it had been ripped off a car. One of the screws meant to hold it was still attached.

Somebody had torn off a license plate and thrown it down toward the river.

Gingerly, he placed it in the largest evidence bag. In his notebook he carefully recorded the spot where he'd found it. It was time to head home—his mother would be worried, and besides, he was hungry.

So off he went with his license plate, a blue and white trophy borne by a little boy in a bright orange hunting vest. Even Tommy Reynolds would be amazed by what his discovery was going to lead to.

"Good heavens, yes, Officer Shoemaker. By all means. If he refused to turn the thing over to you, send him in here to see me. I'll lock him up and throw away the key. Yes, indeed. Send him in."

Captain Fielding Booker was seated at his desk in the small police headquarters in downtown Hamilton. Before him on the desk were copies of all reports filed in the district within the last forty-eight hours; nearly a dozen, which was a high number for Hamilton. But in the last two weeks before Christmas people seemed to lose perspective, to forget the difference between what they wanted and what they actually needed. It was madness—great for commerce, but bad for the crime rate. It made Booker depressed, all these burglaries. The worst was the report he had just been reading—the theft of four boxes of toys purchased by local schoolchildren and destined for a home for disabled orphans in New York City. The shipment had been a class project of the entire fifth grade at the Jefferson School, and someone had stolen the boxes right out of the Hamilton Post Office. Fielding Booker shook his head sadly. Even in

Hamilton, it seemed that standards were shot to hell.

He looked up and scowled as Tommy Reynolds entered the office. Ordinarily, Booker wasn't much given to socializing with children. They found his formality disconcerting, because in their world decorum was, for the most part, merely a thing encountered in strange stories from another age. But Booker had to admit (privately, to himself alone) that Tommy Reynolds wasn't too bad. He had let Tommy borrow a silk top hat for yesterday's performance; evidently the boy had come to return it. Booker wouldn't mind spending a few minutes with him.

"Good morning, sir," said Tommy politely.

"Good morning." Booker gestured to his work. "I've got quite a busy morning ahead of me, young man. I imagine you've come to return my top hat."

"Um, yes, sir," said Tommy, handing Booker a large brown twine-handled paper bag. Booker looked inside; everything seemed to be ship-shape.

"Well, then. Suppose you run along." Booker tried to sound genial, but his temper got in the way. He only succeeded in sounding impatient. Instantly he felt a little guilty.

"Um—I have a question. Sir."

"Yes?" Booker tried to sound interested.

Tommy reached into the small blue backpack

slung over his shoulder and produced his evidence bag containing the license plate. "What should I do with this?"

Booker squinted. "A Connecticut license plate? Can't say. Start yourself a collection. When I was young, my friend Ed Daley had all forty-eight states, and Panama." Booker attempted a cordial smile, but Tommy wasn't buying.

Tommy looked perplexed. "Don't you want to trace it?"

"Now, why would I want to tie up a lot of manpower and telephone time doing something like that?"

"Oh. I only thought—"

"Tell you what. I'll let you in on a little secret that experienced police officers know all about. Most people, when they lose something like this, don't care too much. Too lazy, really. The people who lost this plate, now, you take my word for it, they'll just order up a new one from the Department of Motor Vehicles. Or, if they're really lazy, they'll go without it until they're caught."

"But how would anybody lose a—"

"Appreciate the effort, young fellow. Now, as you can see, I've got quite a lot of work to do. Suppose you just take your license plate and run along."

"Yes, sir." Tommy knew a bullheaded grownup when he met one. He never bothered to try to wear them down; a frontal attack didn't usually work, and only made him tired. He would think of some way to go around Captain Booker, that was all. "Thank you for letting me use the hat."

Already hatching another plan, Tommy headed away from the police station happily enough. His mother would be picking him up at Josie's Place in fifteen minutes, but he knew she would want to order a cup of coffee and sit and talk to whoever was there. The library was right around the corner. He would have time to change his book, have a consultation with Mrs. James, and even pick up new batteries for his flashlight.

He was quite a strategist, was Tommy Reynolds.

A few minutes after Tommy left police head-quarters Officer Kate Shoemaker appeared at Booker's door with a sheet of paper in her hand. She was on communications duty this morning, which meant mostly listening to static on the radio. But she also received the routine reports as they came in, wrote them up on the proper form (HP-CR), and turned a duplicate copy in to Booker.

"This one just in over the fax machine, sir," she said in a bored voice. "A stolen vehicle."

"Bloody hell!" exclaimed Booker. "Don't these people ever rest?"

Kate Shoemaker, not wanting to catch the

captain's wrath, slipped the paper on top of his desk and ducked out.

It was a full twenty minutes before Booker took a look at the report. When he did, he saw that the vehicle in question was a rental car, a four-door sedan, that had been rented on the previous Thursday to a V. Salgo. That was the Jeff's headmaster, or, he supposed, ex-head. Fielding Booker was too busy with the pre-Christmas crime wave to have given much thought to the squabbling of a bunch of privileged academics. The police captain lived in the real world, without the insulation conferred by prestigious institutions—shielded only by his badge, his honor, and his dedication to the citizenry of Hamilton. The thought of so much nobility and integrity brought him momentarily close to tears. He returned his attention to the paper before him. He had no time for self-indulgence.

Yet this was how they repaid him—even the supposedly reputable members of his community weren't above careless mischief. Salgo had signed a contract for only twenty-four hours, and the clerk—in violation of the rules—had accepted a cash payment in lieu of a credit card. Well, the clerk had been negligent, but then again, Salgo was a prominent citizen.

Or had been, before his sudden (some said forced) departure from the Jefferson School.

Well, thought Fielding Booker, donning an

old homburg and a gray loden cape, that was the least of his worries. He was far more concerned with the stolen toys. This was Christmas, dash it all! He wasn't going to let that one rest.

He slid the stolen-car report to the bottom of a pile, pausing briefly to note a curious small coincidence.

But then again, maybe not so curious. Rental cars can be registered in any state, after all.

10

"I THINK WE'VE created a monster, George," remarked Rigton Blair. The two men were having lunch in the Hamilton Club; George knew for certain what Murray Hill had merely surmised, that it was just about the only place in town that Rigton Blair knew how to find.

George had been a member in his youth, before his marriage, but his wife, Lois, had refused to countenance his belonging to an all-male club. She had been a great egalitarian, had Lois, and in the early days of their marriage George had often struggled against the complacency that he believed, in his heart, to be a man's natural state. She waited for nobody, and he had adored her. Not even at the end had she waited for him, but had gone on her own, unafraid and cheerful in spite of the cancer.

Today was the first time he had darkened the

door of the Hamilton Club since saying "I will"
nearly forty years ago. Today he had mentally
offered Lois a swift, laughing apology on his
way through the marble-clad foyer. But there
wasn't another place that Rigton Blair had ever
been known to lunch in; and if you were the
richest man in town, and the crustiest, and
inclined to think a great deal of yourself, then
the Hamilton Club probably was right for you.
At least, that's how George saw it.

"What do you mean, a monster?" he asked.
He was picking gingerly at his lunch, noting
happily that the menu—the Gentlemen's Buffet,
it was called—hadn't changed in four decades:
overdone pork roast on Tuesdays, with green
beans and mashed potatoes, and for dessert,
browbeaten baked apples served with antique
hard sauce. It was all laid out on the long buffet
table, and the sight of it had instantly put
George in mind of Miss Havisham and her
wedding cake. Thank heaven he had learned to
cook.

"I mean this." Blair took a swallow of his
wine, wiped his lips carefully, and gazed sternly
at George. "That dreadful Sanderson woman."

"The Acting Head? The board faces no problem with her." Rigton Blair looked unconvinced,
so George went on. "It's purely temporary, her
appointment. We can replace her at any time.
What's the problem?"

"The problem is that she's ambitious, and

she's shrewd, and she's got everybody's number."

George gave him a blank stare, which Blair apparently found annoying. "Don't go all innocent on me, George. I heard about the way she approached you yesterday evening in the library."

"She spoke to me, certainly," admitted George, recalling the conversation he'd had with the battleaxe on Monday. She had borne down on him and said something mysterious and coy about their both being on the same team. He had merely smiled at her, certain that she was trying to drum up support for a permanent appointment as headmistress, and equally certain that he would never endorse her candidacy. Then he changed the subject to the early life of Charles Dickens, a topic in which she could not feign interest—and so she drifted off. At the time, George had been rather proud of the way he'd managed to get rid of the woman without offending her.

"She did more than speak to you, George."

"Good heavens, Rigton, what are you getting at?"

"George, let's be men about this. Don't play the innocent. You're in a vulnerable position—a widower, probably a bit lonely. And then an attractive woman like Leticia Sanderson puts herself in your path." Blair raised his eyebrows, as if to say "Eh? Eh?"

George contained his mirth, although it wasn't easy. Rigton Blair evidently thought the Sanderson woman attractive—or at least believed that another man might find her so, which amounted, more or less, to the same thing. There was nothing really unattractive about Leticia Sanderson, physically, but her permanent scowl and the look of keen ambition in her eyes made George want to run like a rabbit when he saw her.

The only thing to do was to answer Blair in an equivalently serious way. Then the subject would be considered closed—Blair would have issued his "word to the wise," like some fictional British colonel posted to India, and no doubt would feel that he need never again caution George on this matter.

"You needn't be concerned, Rigton," said George, trying to sound like a subordinate officer. "There will be no hint of impropriety. My honor, as a matter of fact, would not permit it."

"Glad to hear it. Shall we get ourselves some dessert?" Blair rose and nodded to the waiter, who nodded to a red-jacketed busboy, who scurried over to clear their plates. Blair led the way to the buffet table. "Do a damned good baked apple in the kitchen here. Nothing wrong with fruit for dessert. Don't know why all the younger folk go on and on about ice cream and that God-awful yogurt stuff. Give me a good baked apple at the club, any day."

George, sure they *would* give it to Blair any day, merely nodded and selected his apple from the dozen or so set out in a long cut-glass dish.

When they were seated again, Blair opened a new topic of conversation. "Now. Has that young man gotten any further in tracking down that scoundrel Salgo?"

"No, not so far as I've heard, anyway. I talked to him yesterday, of course, at the library. He told me Salgo still hasn't turned up."

"Damn and blast," said Blair, in a curiously flat tone.

"But as I've told you before, Rigton, I really don't think you need worry. That letter will stand up, because the board can be considered, first and foremost, to be 'concerned' in such a thing. 'To Whom It May Concern' *ipso facto, a priori* includes the board."

"I still don't like it, George. We've got to get that joker to sign a proper letter of resignation. Then I'll rest easy."

George took a mouthful of baked apple and gave the matter some thought. Rigton Blair was, to say the least, not an easygoing fellow, but it seemed to George that he was worked up to a disproportionate degree about Salgo. Still, the Jeff was more or less his progeny, in a way. It had been built, originally, with Blair dollars and maintained for a century with endowments, grants, loans, and gifts from the Blair counting-house. It was unlikely that Blair, now over sixty years old and still a bachelor, would ever marry. In all probability he was contemplating an enormous bequest to the school.

If only the man had something other than money to offer. Good sense, good humor, solid leadership for the Board of Trustees—but all Blair had was his fortune.

George refrained from telling the chairman that his concern was ridiculous, and instead outlined a plan that he felt the board could safely follow in the event that Salgo tried to reclaim his job. Over coffee and brandy, the two men discussed local politics and the Town Council's plan to raise water rates, and they parted on a friendly enough note.

But George was a little perturbed. He resolved to tell Dewey of his concerns tomorrow, over a delicious dinner of baked sole. For now, however, there were other matters requiring his attention. More or less retired from practice before the bar, George found there was still a substantial demand for his legal expertise, and he kept a small office on the third floor of the Grain Merchants Building, where he spent a dozen hours each week. It was here now that he bent his steps, resisting the temptation to call in at the library as he passed its welcoming door. Dewey had probably already left for home, anyway, he reasoned.

But Dewey hadn't left the library; she was ensconced in her office with Tommy Reynolds, looking over the evidence.

Although Dewey would have been hard-pressed to say exactly what the Connecticut license plate testified to, still she felt that Tommy had displayed an admirable mixture of curiosity and scientific understanding, both in the means of exploring the place where he'd seen the light, and in his careful preservation of the license plate in a clean freezer bag. This was a boy who could go far indeed, if he got the encouragement from the adult world that he so obviously craved. Therefore, unlike her friend and sometime adversary, Fielding Booker, Dewey took the license plate seriously.

"Captain Booker said it probably fell off," Tommy was saying, "but it was halfway down Johnson's Ravine. I think somebody threw it down there."

Dewey looked the plate over carefully, making sure not to touch it. There was a screw still attached in one of the little holes at the top; close inspection showed that the threads were torn.

"Too bad I don't have a magnifying glass here," she said.

"Here, use mine." Tommy hurriedly fumbled in his backpack for his Swiss Army knife, and proudly unfolded the magnifier.

"Impressive," murmured Dewey. She peered through the glass for a convincingly long time, then returned it to Tommy. "It doesn't look as if it's been lying around for a long time. Rather clean."

"Well, there was snow on it, but that melted." Tommy looked inside the freezer bag, where indeed there was a little puddle in one corner. "But it didn't have any leave or grass or dirt on it."

"Which would make me think, Tommy, that it had only been there a few days."

"Since the night I saw the light!"

Dewey, eager to keep Tommy away from the Goose Bumps and Stephen King, nodded her head gravely at the possibility. "There's certainly a chance of that," she agreed.

"But then," Tommy mused, half to himself, "how come I didn't see lights on the road? How come all I saw was somebody in the woods? I mean if they were looking for it in their car . . ." His voice trailed off, and a frown crossed his brow. This would take some thinking.

"What should I do, Mrs. James?"

"I'd say you should hold on to it. Perhaps the owners will advertise in the *Quill*. You never know."

"No, guess not." Tommy shouldered his backpack, thanked Dewey, and went out front to wait for his mother.

Dewey was getting ready to go home when she was struck by a thought. She glanced at her watch—nearly two. Fielding Booker should be having his lunch at Josie's Place right now, according to his unvarying custom. Perfect.

She put on her coat, said goodbye to Tom Campbell, and headed out the door. Sergeant Mike Fenton would be on duty at the police station. He adored Dewey, and would do almost anything for her—except defy direct orders. But Dewey felt certain that a little investigative work wouldn't interfere with his obligations—Captain Booker need never know.

11

When George arrived home that afternoon and checked his answering machine, he was not really surprised to hear a message from Sandra Albee. His first impulse was to erase it—Sandra never called unless she wanted something, and she still owed George money for some legal work he'd done for her a year or so ago.

But remembering Sandra's place on the Jefferson board, he felt he ought to at least see what she wanted. Besides, if he didn't return her call, she would surely phone again to ask why he'd ignored her message. As George well knew, Sandra was a very persistent woman who nearly always got what she wanted.

What she wanted this afternoon was a cozy little drink with George. She suggested her place, but George had the good sense to insist that they go to the Seven Locks Tavern, which was the most public place in town. People who met on the sly did not go to the Seven Locks. Sandra agreed to meet him there, but it was clear from her tone that she wasn't happy about it.

Thus it was that on that Tuesday evening George found himself out on the town, so to speak, with a very attractive and ambitious woman. It seemed unlikely that Sandra had set her cap for him, so he felt safe enough, in spite of Rigton Blair's worries about his vulnerability as a widower. George knew exactly where his Achilles heel was.

"The thing is," Sandra was saying, over her Pink Lady, "that I feel somehow as if the whole thing is my fault. I mean—Victor Salgo never would have been appointed headmaster in the first place if I hadn't been so *totally* taken in by him. I guess maybe I've learned how to be persuasive in my old age." She paused, laughing modestly, with a "What? Me old??" look on her face. When George failed to respond with the expected compliment, she went on. "Because really it was all my doing. Now I'm afraid that they won't listen to a word I say, and I care so *much* about the Jeff. It's our cultural heritage."

"I wouldn't let it worry you, Sandra," said George, in a no-nonsense tone of voice. She was looking for sympathy, but he didn't feel much like proferring his shoulder. It seemed to him that the crisis at the Jefferson, rather than fading away, was blooming like camellias in Charleston. It was certainly taking up a lot of his time, officially and unofficially, and he was getting a little bit tired of the whole thing. He wished he had the nerve to tell his civic conscience to take a hike.

"The thing is, George," said Sandra, "It *does* worry me. I can't help it. I worry about things." She looked up at him from beneath perfectly mascaraed lashes. Her neat blond hair fell away from her face, revealing gold drop earrings that hung prettily along her delicate throat. As usual her outfit was a perfect blend of light, bright shades: beige suit with an apricot-colored silk blouse, pale stockings, and beige high-heeled shoes. Even in deepest winter, George had never seen her in any color darker than pale fawn. And he had never seen her looking less than impeccable. He wondered idly how much of her day she devoted to putting together The Look. Probably by now she was an expert and could look perfect in under thirty minutes.

Briefly an image of Dewey flashed through George's mind—Dewey with her silvery curls that were never in place, dressed in her bulky old purple sweater over a practical black turtleneck, a sensible skirt, boots to keep out the winter cold. He felt a rush of tenderness, and a smile crossed his face, unbidden.

Sandra Albee jumped at it—surely it was a

smile meant for her alone. She reached out a finger and rested it momentarily, ever so lightly, on George's wrist. "Is it true, what they say, George?"

"What do they say?" George removed his hand from her reach to signal the barman, Nils Reichart, for another round.

"That he flew the coop."

"Who? Victor Salgo?" George didn't want to talk about it with anyone, least of all with Sandra Albee.

"That he just upped and went away. Well— he always was the irresponsible sort, it turns out." Sandra put an elbow on the table and rested her dainty chin on an upraised fist. "There are stories. They say he 'dated'—to put it politely—one of his students, and that she was so traumatized by the whole affair that she's been in a rest home for years. Now she's getting out, and the family is suing. I forget their name—"

"My mother always told me that names and tales don't mix," said George. Ye *gods*, this woman was a gossip.

"So true—except, having heard only now about the man's past, George, I feel responsible. But how was I to know?"

"Thank you, Nils," said George in a loud voice, as their drinks arrived. If the barman noted the relief in George's voice, he didn't let on.

"But one has to be practical," Sandra went on. "I've decided I don't want people to think it's all my fault. So I pick myself up and get back in the race—that's life, right, George?" She sipped carefully at her Pink Lady. "The thing is, George, that we'd better get cracking on finding someone to take Victor's place."

"I imagine that's a procedure that's going to take some time, Sandra," said George. "But there's no rush right now. Best at least to get the second semester underway, with Ms. Sanderson in charge. I'm sure that the board will offer her all the support we can," he added in an admonishing tone, noting the look of *frío* that had crossed Sandra's face at the mention of Leticia Sanderson's name. George could have sworn that Sandra actually bared her teeth. Then again, perhaps he only imagined it.

"Of course we'll support her." Sandra was smiling prettily again. "The thing is, George, that I want to help. But now I feel ostracized. Do you know that Rigton hasn't called me in four days? Don't you think I'm entitled to know what's going on?" There was the trace of a pout about her pink mouth, a practiced *moue*.

George wondered if she rehearsed the pout in a mirror. Probably had, as a young girl. By now it came naturally. "Of course, Sandra, we're all entitled to know. But I doubt that Rigton Blair has anything to tell us."

"But you had lunch with him today."

George gave her a long look. Was this woman spying on him? She read his mind. "I was on my way to Frenell's, and I saw you leaving the Hamilton Club at two o'clock. You're not a member, so you must have been having lunch with Rigton."

"Good reasoning, Sherlock," said George, trying to keep his voice even. "But we weren't there to discuss school business. We talked about the water-rate hearings scheduled for next month." George was a terrible liar, because he almost never got any practice. But on occasion he felt he had no other recourse, and it didn't much matter whether people suspected a lie or not. This was one such occasion. Now, if he could only find a way to get out of there.

Sandra Albee studied him and decided against a direct challenge. She tried another tack: efficiency. She was famous for it, after all. "It doesn't matter, anyway." She waved away his untruth. "The thing is, George, I'd like to move forward. We have a regularly scheduled board meeting on January fourth, and I think it would be smart to try to reach a consensus before then, so we don't have to spend hours wrangling with everyone. That's such a bore."

George, too, found wrangling a bore, but he thought that's what being a board member was all about: debate. "A consensus about what?"

"About the future of the Jeff."

"You know, Sandra," said George, beginning

to lose his temper, "my place on the board is only temporary, until April, when the next round of board elections will be held. So I'm not certain I'll even be on hand to take part in selecting the new head for the school."

"Yes, but you have a voice, George. The thing is, I don't really have one." She gave him a kittenish smile. "That's why I wanted to talk to you, in private. So that I could tell you my idea. People always listen to you, George."

"Not always," he demurred, scenting danger.

"And I thought it would be really wonderful if we could work as a team. Interestingly, I almost always agree with you, you know. So if maybe we could develop a shared point of view at the meetings, I think that would help get our message across, don't you? I thought it would be nice to keep in touch that way."

George had had enough. He looked at his watch, made a casual excuse about a dinner engagement, and signaled to Nils Reichart for the bill. The burly Swede flicked George the shadow of a smile; George felt certain this wasn't the first time Nils had witnessed some poor man trying to avoid the web Sandra Albee liked to spin. He paid the bill, and without apology, left her unceremoniously at her front door. Feeling better, he headed home, where he took a long hot shower and spent a solid five minutes studying himself in the mirror. All he saw was a respectable, graying man; handsome enough, certainly, for his age, but that was nothing. He could live with himself, and sleep well at night. Those were the things that counted with George.

What had she thought she would find here, that Albee woman?

And, come to think of it, why *had* she offered to "work as a team" with him?

He must be giving off pheromones, like some kind of overgrown ant, he decided. Depressed, George poured himself a nightcap of Cointreau and climbed into bed with a dog-eared copy of the *Meditations* of Marcus Aurelius. But for once that practical and insightful philosopher failed to soothe. After a long while, George slept, but uneasily, and dreamed of well-clad chambermaids armed with large cans of Raid.

Like George, Dewey was having trouble settling down to sleep that night, but she had worries other than apparent irresistibility for the opposite sex.

It seemed to Dewey that there were just too many things going on.

For starters, there was Christmas around the corner, her daughter coming, presents and trees and caroling, and all sorts of things to be thought about. Dewey had been debating all week between baking a mince pie and ordering a fancy plum pudding, and she still hadn't made up her mind.

On top of all of that, there was the more immediate and disturbing question of Tommy Reynolds and his "evidence." Dewey had been giving a lot of thought, one way and another, to Tommy's evidence.

She sat up in her old four-poster, wrapped in a thick satin quilt, sipping hot tea, and thinking. Her large black Labrador retriever, Isaiah, had made himself at home at the foot of the bed and was snoring loudly. Ordinarily he was not permitted to sleep on the bed, but for reasons beyond her present understanding, Dewey had relaxed this rule tonight. Maybe I'm lonely, she thought. Plain old lonely. But she didn't *feel* lonely. She felt quite content, as a rule, at peace with herself and the world.

Her daughter, Grace, would be home in four days' time, but only for the long Christmas weekend—she'd fly in on the red-eye from San Diego, changing in Cincinnati for the puddle-jumper to Hamilton. It was a long trip, and an expensive one, but Grace liked to be home at Christmas. She always told her mother that this was because she missed the cold weather in Hamilton; Dewey hoped she missed her mother, too, and some of her friends.

Dewey had decided to have a little party in Grace's honor—just eggnog and cookies in the parlor, for a handful of Grace's schoolmates (the few who remained in Hamilton) and some of Dewey's close friends. This afternoon she had

done a very atypical thing; she had behaved like
a mother; she had called Murray Hill, that "nice
young man from the Jeff," and invited him to
come for eggnog. Dewey had no illusions, but
she wasn't above fantasizing from time to time.
And (Grace knew only too well) Dewey did
have a knack for Orchestrating Things. Grace's
visit was to be so short that it was no good
leaving such a thing to chance.

But that was all still many days away. Dewey
had bigger fish to fry at the moment, because
Mike Fenton had called her late this evening with
news. The license plate that Tommy Reynolds
found had been traced to a rental car that had
been reported stolen only this afternoon. Fenton
had instantly gone to Booker with the news of
an anonymous lead on the stolen vehicle, where-
upon Booker, filled with righteous anger, had
blown his stack. He didn't give a fig (he had
said, with mighty thunder in his voice) about
some blasted rental car that had stayed out past
its curfew. In a fury of the Christmas spirit, he
forbade his men (including Kate Shoemaker) to
investigate any (expletive) stolen car. He or-
dered them to round-the-clock duty tracking
those toys stolen from the post office. So, Mike
apologized to Dewey for not being able to make
better use of her lead—and promised that
he would call in a day or two, "when we get the
Barbies and the Z-Bots rounded up."

Well, poor Mike—Dewey knew that he probably had all kinds of family commitments just at this time, but that was what you had to expect when you had a policeman in the family. She knew; her late husband, Brendan, who had been Fielding Booker's predecessor as captain of the Hamilton Police, had often needed to absent himself from family life. It hadn't been easy, even in those days, and the crime rate in Hamilton had more than doubled over the last ten years. Booker and his staff would be kept busy.

Which meant, Dewey now reasoned, that it was her duty to do what she could to help them. They would appreciate her effort when they learned about it, which wouldn't be until she had found a few answers. It was just too bad she hadn't managed to get a little bit more information out of Mike Fenton—but she had enough to go on.

She reached for the telephone book from the bottom shelf of the night table and turned to the listings of car rental agencies. There were only six in the greater Hamilton area; since the license plate was from out of state, Dewey reasoned that the car must have come from one of the three national chains represented here. That narrowed things considerably. She jotted the telephone numbers down on a piece of paper and glanced at the clock. Nearly ten, but it was worth a try. All those companies ran their businesses out of computerized central switchboards somewhere—Dewey always assumed it was Atlanta, but she didn't know why.

On the second call, she struck pay dirt. Satisfied, she made one more call, and fell asleep, happily contemplating her task for tomorrow.

12

Excited at the prospect of proving Tommy Reynolds a hero, Dewey had slept well. After talking to the car rental agency, she had called Tommy last night, explaining that she thought his evidence might be the lead necessary to track a stolen car. With the approval of Tommy's parents, Dewey and the boy had scheduled a rendezvous for first light. Her idea was to reconnoiter the place where Tommy had found the license plate, and then to go with the evidence, and Tommy, to the rental office nearby. The company would probably be grateful; they might even offer a reward, although Dewey hadn't mentioned this possibility to Tommy.

She rose before six, fed and watered Starbuck, gave Isaiah an extra helping of kibble, and was headed for the Reynolds' house just as the sun was coming up behind Summer Ridge.

Tommy was waiting at the end of the driveway, knapsack slung over one shoulder, shifting from foot to foot to keep out the cold. He looked still half asleep, his soft blond hair sticking out every which way, his eyes a little unfocused. But he was alert, asking Dewy to go over, once more, what she had learned from the police and the car rental agency.

Dewey explained again as her old station wagon bounced inelegantly down the long hill toward Cutter's Lane, over the narrow, open-grid bridge, and up onto Route 52. But as they approached the spot Tommy grew silent, looking carefully out the window.

"A little further—wait, slow down, slow *down*—there, okay, stop!"

Dewey stopped where Tommy bid her, and the two got out of the car.

In the cold half-light the spot looked about as deserted as anywhere within fifty miles of Hamilton. It wasn't a very attractive place, the terrain uninviting, with the large swath of burned-over ground and a few unappealingly jagged boulders breaking the landscape here and there. Dewey looked up and down the road. It seemed an utterly desolate place, the only evidence of habitation the bits of anonymous-looking plastic, the soggy remnants of beer six-packs, and scrags of foil wrappers that littered the scene.

From where Dewey and Tommy stood, the descent toward the Boone River was steep; to the right and left, where the woods still stood, there would be trees to break your fall if you slipped—but not here. Dewey was glad she had put on her boots instead of her sneakers.

"Do me a favor, Tommy," she told him. "Don't fall down that hill."

"Don't worry, Mrs. James," the boy replied, in a serious voice. Tommy knew a fall would be dangerous. "But look, we can go that way." He pointed to the right, where a trail led into the woods from the road. "It's dry in there, too."

They made their way along the trail, which wound gently downhill for about seventy-five yards. Tommy stopped at one spot and pointed through the trees to the left.

"The license plate was over there. Kind of in the middle. I have it in my notes." He gestured to the knapsack.

In another minute or so, they reached a place where a large, flat boulder jutted outward, creating a mossy terrace. From this point, the ground fell away too steeply for them to advance farther. It was a fifty-yard drop to the river, nearly straight down.

Tommy, all eagerness, took his binoculars from his knapsack. He lay down on his belly and elbow-crawled forward until his head and shoulders were beyond the edge of the boulder. He lifted the binoculars to his eyes, squinted, adjusted. The he lay motionless, looking.

After thirty seconds or so, he whistled. "Wanna look, Mrs. James?"

"Sure." Dewey lay down next to Tommy, and he passed her the binoculars.

It was difficult to make out at first, because of the woody debris on all sides. But finally Dewey brought it into focus: The back end of a black sedan was pointed straight up in the air, its chassis stuck, apparently, on a large rock, or maybe a tree trunk. The car, from what Dewey could estimate, lay more or less directly below the burned-over area. There was no license plate on the rear bumper.

"Good work, Tommy," she said, her blue eyes shining with excitement. "Let's go."

"Do you think there's a reward?" asked Tommy, trying to sound casual.

"Probably," said Dewey, vowing to see that there was a reward, one way or another.

"Who the devil—?" muttered Fielding Booker. He padded down the hall in his bedroom slippers, his mind fuzzy with sleep. It was unthinkable that anybody would ring his doorbell at seven in the morning. His men had strict orders to telephone first. The only person in town with the temerity to come calling at this hour was Dewey James, but Booker couldn't imagine what on earth even she could want. Lately she had been leaving him in peace, although Booker had a dread suspicion that the hiatus was too good to last. With a shudder he considered the possibilities. Probably she had decided to lend her dubious assistance to the matter of the stolen toys.

He raised his eyes briefly in supplication, but his prayer went unanswered.

As Booker opened his front door, Tommy Reynolds nearly forgot what he had come for. For weeks he had seen Hamilton's captain of police in nightshirt and old-fashioned nightcap, got up as Scrooge. But here was Fielding Booker in real life—in a nightshirt, thick flannel dressing gown, and long, pompommed woolen nightcap. The sight was almost too much for the boy. Dewey, however, was accustomed to her friend's sartorial eccentricities. She was amused (never having surprised him in his night clothes before), but not astounded at the get-up. It was a look that suited him admirably, she thought.

"Dewey! What in heaven's name are you doing here?" Booker glowered at Tommy, pointing an accusing finger. "Don't tell me you put him up to it. As if it isn't enough to try to cope with my workload, now I've got this young scamp coming to my office all the blessed day, bothering me and my staff with his Boy Scout fantasies—"

"Now, Fielding Booker!" Dewey cut in sharply.

"There is no cause for you to be rude and insulting just because you got up on the wrong side of the bed this morning. It's high time you were up, anyway. Do you intend to go on shivering on your doorstep? Or may we come in?"

Booker swallowed his ill temper and ushered them in. Sulking, he led them to the kitchen, where Tommy sat thunderstruck with excitement while Dewey made a large pot of coffee and upbraided Booker further for insulting him. "As a matter of fact," she said firmly, "you should be very grateful to this young man. He's just solved a case for you."

Booker groaned inwardly. It was bad enough that his friend Dewey sought to intrude, repeatedly, in the business of the Hamilton police. Booker was never sure whether she felt she had the right—as the widow of the former police captain—or whether she felt it was somehow her civic duty to be a pest, a gadfly, and a public nuisance. In any event, intrude she did. Her habit of sticking her nose into police business had grown so strong that recently she had even interfered with the activity of the New York City police. Not to mention the effect she'd had on that poor sheriff out West.

Of course, Booker would have to admit that the NYPD had been grateful, and Sheriff Tate, too. They didn't know any better, he reasoned.

But now, to top it all off, Dewey was evidently

training a new generation of meddlesome amateur sleuths. Booker wouldn't have it—not on his patch, as the Chief Inspectors said in England. At seven in the morning, however, in nightshirt and slippers, he felt he somehow lacked the authority to set Dewey straight on this point.

Besides, as Dewey related the tale, he began to think that there was probably something to it. He listened first with impatience—for he knew from long experience that Dewey wouldn't go away until she had had her say. Gradually he grew willing, grudgingly, to admit that the license plate might belong to the car at the bottom of Johnson's Ravine.

"Well, then," prompted Dewey, pointing toward the telephone. "Don't you think you'd better investigate?"

Booker sat back and crossed his arms, regarding Dewey closely. He was mulling over his strategy. He ought to make a call here and now to Mike Fenton, to organize getting the car out of the ravine. However, he wanted Dewey out of his hair, and he especially didn't want her turning up to watch the salvage operation. He considered possibilities for a few moments, and decided that a stitch in time was called for.

"Tell you what, Dewey. I will call. But I feel I must extract a promise from the two of you." He regarded Tommy with as much authority as he could muster in a dressing gown and nightcap. "No further exploration of that site, young man. It is strictly off limits."

Tommy, who had held his tongue with admirable restraint throughout the interview, was compelled to protest. "But, Captain—"

"No, sir. You heard me." He wagged a finger at the two of them. "Dewey, you should know better than to permit your young friend to go poking around in such a dangerous spot. He might fall and hurt himself."

Dewey refrained from pointing out that she had nothing to do with Tommy's initial visit to the place. Instead she gave Tommy a squeeze on the shoulder as he started once more to protest, and stood up. "We promise," she said soothingly to Booker.

Mollified, he reached for the phone and dialed poor Mike Fenton at home. If the young sergeant was surprised by his superior's early-morning call about the stolen vehicle—a case that only yesterday had been labeled lowest-priority—he didn't say so. He naturally wondered (given his conversation yesterday with Dewey) how much dotty old Mrs. James had to do with the change in orders; but Mike, by means of his native tact, had survived with Booker for a long time, so he kept his mouth shut. He would have a chance later to talk to Mrs. James if the car turned out to be the same one.

*   *   *

"Captain Booker sure wasn't very nice about things," remarked Tommy as Dewey drove him back to his house.

"You have to make allowances, Tommy."

"Why?" Tommy was bitterly disappointed. Far from being a hero, he had been labeled a pest by the very person who ought most to have appreciated his effort.

"Well, for one thing, we surprised him in his nightshirt, which probably made him feel funny—"

"Yeah, but I've been seein' his nightshirt for two weeks now at rehearsal."

"Yes," agreed Dewey thoughtfully, "but that's different. He was in *costume* then."

The distinction evidently was lost on Tommy, who put one foot on the opposite knee, pulled his Swiss Army knife from his backpack, and began to carve at the sole of his boot.

"There's a saying, Tommy: 'No good deed goes unpunished.'"

"Yeah, great."

"Well, I'll let you in on a little secret."

"Yeah?"

"You will probably have to give evidence. In a interview called a deposition."

"Not if *he* has anything to do with it," said Tommy, but there was hope in his voice.

"Of course you will. You'll need your notebook and everything. And you just may have to reenact your discovery."

Tommy was far from satisfied, but he had recovered some of his good humor by the time they arrived at his door. He had a smile for Dewey, at least. It wasn't until he was inside his house that he realized that Fielding Booker had forgotten to ask him for the license plate.

He let out a whoop of laughter, and wondered if Mrs. James knew. Probably.

Mike Fenton stood outside, shifting from one foot to another, his arms wrapped around him. Kate Shoemaker was waiting in the patrol car, but Mike preferred the fresh air. It was better to be miserable for a few minutes in this bone-chilling cold, and get the misery over with. By the time the fire truck arrived, with its special crane rig, Fenton would have forgotten that he was cold.

Following Booker's instructions to the letter, he and Kate had crawled on their bellies out on the flat promontory and gazed down into the ravine. There was indeed a car there, but it would require more than just a standard wrecker. Meantime, the rental agency had been informed, and a representative was on his way from Wardville, about thirty miles distant.

The wind was blowing viciously, and it tore with gusto through the burned-over swath. To Fenton's eye, the place looked exactly right for an accident—a sharp curve, a road with no shoulder, limited visibility because of the steep slope and the curve. There really should have been a guardrail on this curve, but that was just one of the many things, Mike reflected, that probably fell between the cracks of two jurisdictions, Hamilton Township and Palmer County. Or maybe, since Route 52 was a state road, it was the state's responsibility. One thing he did know for sure—everyone would blame everyone else. He only hoped that there was no one in the wreck.

But he knew that such hopes were ridiculous. Of course there was someone there.

And if the stolen-vehicle report was anything to go on, the car had been there for maybe three, four, even five days.

It wasn't a pleasant thought, but any lingering doubts would soon be laid to rest. He could see, down the road about thirty yards, the flashing yellow lights of the approaching fire truck.

13

"YOU DON'T SAY." Rigton Blair's voice was bland, disinterested, giving nothing away.

George Farnham couldn't tell what was going through the man's mind. Perhaps relief, he thought cynically, that Victor Salgo wouldn't be asking for his old job back. George had come here to Blair's office to tell him about the car crash in Johnson's Ravine.

It had taken the fire and police crews the better part of three hours before they finally managed to winch the wrecked car up the hill. The car was a write-off, its only occupant (as everyone feared) still at the wheel, but quite dead.

Booker, predictably, had been annoyed—not so much by the death of a citizen as by the fact that one man's carelessness should get in the way of his (Booker's) police force doing some

137

actual good this Christmas season. Fenton and Shoemaker had been tied up all day with the crane, with people from the rental agency, and all that who-struck-John. Just because one middle-aged academic was driving recklessly and went over a cliff. Who was going to find the stolen Christmas toys, Booker wanted to know, if his entire staff was busy mollycoddling some corporate clown who only cared about fiddling the record for his insurance claim?

Booker, therefore, had gone into a prolonged sulk and refused to have anything to do with the car, its recovery, or the status of its occupant. Stripped of nearly all the manpower he could lay claim to, he had resorted to doing the toy case legwork himself. But it had been a long time since he'd had the pleasure of questioning minor witnesses, and his skills had deserted him. He spent the day bullying harried Post Office employees about the four cardboard boxes bound for New York City. When he was through, he knew no more than when he started, but he had managed to leave behind enough ill will to assure a complete moratorium on the delivery to him of anything but late-payment notices and sweep-stakes entries.

Meantime, the reliable Mike Fenton had been left to manage the situation on Route 52. When a look at the driver's wallet turned up Victor Salgo's name, Fenton had had the good sense to call George Farnham. George, in his capacity as a member of the school board, had come to the windswept hillside and offered a preliminary identification of the body. Fenton had put Kate Shoemaker in charge of tracking down next of kin. George, on leaving the crash site, had hurried to the offices of the Blair National Bank, there to inform the heart and soul of the Jefferson School that its former headmaster was dead.

Rigton Blair's office was at the back of the main banking floor, behind an elaborate brass grillwork that separated the everyday customers from the "individuals of high net worth," who banked personally with Blair. Blair's office, richly furnished with Persian rugs, rosewood and teak chairs and tables, and elaborate carvings and tapestries, had the air of a sultan's palace, with an opulence that (some said) crossed the line separating good taste from that other. George knew for a fact that the furnishings were authentic antiques, and worth a fortune. The style wasn't to his taste, but he wasn't about to criticize. He didn't have to see much of it, anyway, not being one of those persons of high net worth whom Rigton Blair stooped to serve.

Blair had greeted the news of Salgo's death with a coolness that surprised Farnham. He seemed to be giving the matter thought, as though there were something personally bothersome about it; but his face gave no hint of what sort of emotion, if any, the news had generated. His cool gray eyes revealed nothing.

"Well," he said finally, as George maintained a stubborn silence, "that more or less lets the board off the hook."

"Yes and no," said George, feeling a rising anger. George didn't like to be cynical about people. Still less did he like it when his cynicism proved accurate. "At the very least, you know, we'll have to have Robert Gaston take a look at him." Gaston was the medical examiner for Hamilton and the surrounding counties.

Blair scowled. "Whatever for?"

"To determine the cause of death." George kept his tone even.

"Ridiculous. Man drove his car off a cliff, that's all. Holiday season, maybe he'd had a few over at the Seven Locks, who knows? Happens all the time." Blair waved it away. Such deaths weren't worth the Hamilton medical examiner's time, he seemed to say.

"Doesn't matter, Rigton. The rental car operators have requested a full investigation, to which they are legally entitled, to find out whether there has been some sort of malfeasance; there's loss of property involved, and someone will have to pay the bill. So, even if the Jefferson School is going to turn its back on the death of its headmaster—"

"Former headmaster," corrected Blair.

George ignored him. "—then the legitimate

claims of the owner of the vehicle must be settled, and whether that will be done through Salgo's insurance, or the company's, remains to be seen."

"Fine. Go ahead." Blair gave a dismissive wave, as though he were authorizing one of his employees to okay a small-time loan to some person beneath his notice. "Go right ahead."

Farnham was annoyed, but he held his temper in check. After exchanging a few more words with Blair, he left the bank, turning up the velvet collar of his old charcoal-gray Chesterfield, and wrapping a cashmere muffler about his neck. The day was bitterly cold, and it would be dark soon. He headed home, ducking into the wind as it tore up along Slingluff Street, sending dust and bits of debris flying. He glanced at his watch: nearly five, and Dewey was coming to dinner at six. He would have a little bit of time to think, while he made dinner for them. He wanted to talk to Dewey about it, hear her reaction. The whole situation struck him as very, very odd.

"Extraordinary," Dewey commented, accepting another glass of Chardonnay from George. They had finished the sole *à la meunière*, served with new potatoes and a green salad; they had made brisk work of two tiny strawberry shortcakes (George apologizing, the whole way, for the frozen strawberries, although Dewey liked them just fine); they were now finishing a bottle of wine and talking over the remarkable events of the day. Dewey had related her excursion of the morning, and George his forays of the afternoon. "The whole thing, from start to finish, has been extraordinary," Dewey repeated. "The poor man—well, I never knew him, really, but you can't help feeling sorry for him. Do you know, George, that there probably isn't one person in town who cares about his going? Not one."

"It is odd," George agreed. He thought, on the whole, that it would be better to be loathed and detested like Rigton Blair than to leave a wake of indifference behind you. He expressed this sentiment to Dewey, who nodded vigorously.

"Indeed it would, George." She became thoughtful for a moment. "You don't suppose, do you, that he might have killed himself?"

"I do suppose," said George firmly. "Look at the facts, Dewey. First"—he held up a finger—"the man left a very strange note to the school board, and disappeared from sight. Second, there was apparently something in his past that was coming back to haunt him. More than one thing." He told Dewey about the anonymous letter that the school board had received in November, condemning Salgo as "a thief and worse."

"And that's not all," said George. "There was

something else surfacing. The faint whiff of a scandal at the school where he used to teach in New York City."

"Yes, but George, surely—that was seven years ago. More, perhaps."

"I have the feeling it was coming back to torment him, whatever it was."

"Dear me," said Dewey sympathetically. "What kind of scandal?"

"Involving a young woman, I gather." George recounted what he knew, including (decently censored) an account of his evening at the Seven Locks with Sandra Albee, and her curiosity about the matter. "She wanted to know all about it."

"Lascivious, maybe," suggested Dewey.

"Maybe," agreed George.

"Or perhaps she thought the information could be useful to her," said Dewey, looking thoughtful.

"How so?"

"I don't know, George. But I'll tell you one thing. Fielding Booker has declined, absolutely, to show any interest in this situation."

"And?" asked George, with a note of fondness in his voice.

"Well, George, the answer is evident. It's up to the two of us, as usual."

So pleased was George with the way Dewey had put this notion that he didn't remonstrate at all.

Besides, for once in his life George felt like prying into someone else's affairs. Victor Salgo might have been a bad headmaster, and perhaps he was in trouble. But no man ought to kill himself. George wanted to know why.

14

"THAT GUITAR IS bothering me," said Dewey firmly to Isaiah. It was Wednesday morning, and a brilliant winter sun was warming Dewey's kitchen and the small pasture beyond. She sat in her favorite chair, looking out the window, with her slippered feet propped against Isaiah's warm back. It was on mornings like this one that she was especially grateful to be working only part time, when she could sit over a second cup of coffee and contemplate the sunrise over the wintry blown landscape that she loved so well. Very quickly, however, her contemplation this morning had shifted from the landscape to the more intriguing matter of Victor Salgo's death.

Perhaps George was right; perhaps the man had driven himself over the cliff deliberately. But it seemed an odd way to commit suicide; and

Dewey felt, somehow, that the picture didn't fit. Something about it was off.

If it had been an accident, it had certainly taken place at just the right spot. Twenty yards farther in either direction were trees, large enough and sturdy enough to keep a car from plunging down the ravine; but just here, in that funny broad patch of burned-over ground, was there room for a car to go straight down.

George and Mike Fenton had discussed the need for a guardrail; but really, Dewey mused, the angle of the curve wasn't so sharp that most drivers would be in any danger. In fact, she held up her hands on an imaginary steering wheel, using Isaiah as accelerator, brake, and clutch, and closed her eyes. She visualized herself driving on Route 52. If you were coming from the direction of the dump (excuse me, sanitary landfill, she thought disparagingly), then you would have to turn your wheel sharply to the left to hit that swath in just the right way to go straight down the hill.

If you were heading the other way, coming from the Cutter's Lane bridge, you'd have to turn right, a hard right. Even so, your car would most likely head down the swath at a diagonal, and you'd run into trees before plunging down the ravine.

So, if it was an accident, it was an unusual one, and Victor Salgo had been mighty unlucky in his rented car that night.

George had made a great deal of the fact that Salgo had been driving a rented car, which certainly did seem odd. Although fond of her own old station wagon, Dewey was not a lover of cars. She couldn't comprehend the idea of someone's taking his own life but making sure that his silver BMW survived. Dewey's active imagination suggested an alternative point of view. "Because I just don't see that buisness about the car that way," she said aloud to Isaiah, as she explained her idea.

The dog, ever a good listener, sighed and opened one eye to gaze upon his mistress. Then he went back to his doggy half-sleep, and Dewey took up the thread of her musings once more.

Half an hour later, she had made up her mind. First she called Franklin Lowe, who had already heard the news about Victor Salgo. "I thought you might want to get your guitar back," she sad, "before things get complicated."

"Dewey, are you up to something?"

"I'm only thinking of you, Franklin. Shall I arrange it?"

"By all means." He agreed to meet her in half an hour, and in the meantime she called George.

"I need your permission for something."

"My dear," said George, delighted that she had called, "never in your life have you asked permission. For anything."

"No, seriously, George. I need your actual,

official, permission. I want to go inside Victor Salgo's house."

"Now just a blessed second, my dear." Dewey, as usual, had sprung ahead by leaps and bounds. "Whatever for?"

"Let's just say I'm nosy," replied Dewey evasively.

"I'm sure nobody would ever accuse you of that, Dewey," said George with a chuckle. "What makes you think I can authorize such a thing?"

"Because. You're on the board. The house belongs to the school. You can do it."

George thought about it. He had already had conversations that morning with both Fielding Booker and Rigton Blair. Both of them seemed so blasé about Salgo's death that George was beginning to feel someone had to take the bull by the horns, if only to show some interest in how and why the poor man had died. Blair, unenthusiastic, had nonetheless told George to "do whatever was strictly necessary." In this case, George decided, Dewey's scheme, whatever it was, qualified.

"All right, my dear. Consider permission granted. But won't you fill me in a little bit?" George sounded hurt.

"Later, George. When I have something concrete to tell you."

She hung up, made a hasty call to the school secretary Vivian Freshet, who was known as

Vivian the Vivacious, and was said to know everything. Two minutes later, Dewey threw on her heavy parka, and was on her way. The house was less than a mile from Dewey's, through the woods, and she was there in fifteen minutes.

Franklin Lowe was waiting for her in Victor Salgo's driveway. Despite the bitter cold he wore only a turtleneck under his leather jacket, which was unzipped halfway. Dewey couldn't imagine riding a motorcycle on such a cold morning; but then again, Dewey had never really cared for the idea whatever the time of year. Give her a horse any day.

"You're a peach, Dew. I knew you could rig it." Franklin greeted her with an affectionate smooch.

Dewey gave him a cautious smile. "Don't you ever tell anyone this was my idea, Franklin. Please."

"On my honor as a gladiator," he replied, holding up his fingers in what Dewey guesses must be some kind of Roman salute.

The spare key was right where Vivian had said it would be, hidden under a rock behind a box bush. Dewey and Franklin picked up the mail—now more than five days' worth—from inside the storm door, and went on inside.

The house had that unmistakable quiet of a place whose occupant is not coming back. But it didn't take Dewey more than a minute to conclude that Salgo had in fact intended to return.

Accident, then. Or something else.

While Franklin Lowe looked for his guitar, Dewey made a rapid but eagle-eyed inspection of the premises. The house was a solid brick structure, fifty years old or so, that the school had bought for the use of its headmaster. It was designed for a family, with four bedrooms upstairs, plenty of bathrooms, and a large backyard. The living room was spacious, and there was a well-stocked library off to one side, a smaller den on the other. The dining room, too, was big. The whole house was attractively furnished with antiques that the school had acquired over the years. It would be a nice perk to live here, especially if you had been scraping by on a teacher's salary for years.

Dewey looked around the library and den carefully, trying to distinguish what might have belonged to Salgo from the things that the school owned. To her way of thinking, the furniture and even the books in the library had an anonymous air. The only palpable difference seemed to be in the items on top of the large teak desk in the corner. A quick look showed Dewey a pile of correspondence, bills to pay, and memos from teachers and administrators. On one corner there was a photograph, unframed, of a group of hairy-looking young people at some kind of picnic or festival. The people in the picture were unknown to Dewey; one, however, struck a chord; a tall, bespectacled woman with long blond braids, dressed in the Indian-print cotton that had been the uniform for young women of an earlier generation. Woodstock, maybe? Dewey thought so, but she had to admit she was an old fogey. She wouldn't know Woodstock if she fell over it.

Dewey moved on. The kitchen, neat and spare and suitable for a bachelor, revealed that Salgo had had company on his last night in the house. There were two wineglasses on the kitchen table, a half-full bottle of Cabernet Sauvignon, and a partly eaten round of Camembert with some forlorn-looking French bread.

Dewey went upstairs, where she found Franklin Lowe in one of the spare bedrooms. He had located his guitar and was sitting on the edge of the bed, looking it over carefully.

"Everything all right?" Dewey asked brightly.

"Shipshape," replied Lowe. "I don't think he even got a chance to practice with it, because it still has the open tuning that I was using last week." He strummed, and even Dewey's only moderately musical ear could tell that it didn't sound like a "regular" guitar.

"Hmm," she said. "Tell me again why he borrowed it?"

"For the Winter Pageant. He had to accompany the fourth grade in a song about a snowman who'd lost his hat."

"Oh." That didn't sound very promising to Dewey.

"There's a rule that everybody, absolutely everybody, has to take part in the pageant, even if it's only a little part. All the students and all the faculty."

"Well, that makes sense, I guess."

"Listen, Dewey," said Lowe, putting the guitar back in its case, "thanks for doing this for me." He gave her a twinkly smile and patted the guitar case. "Any chance I can take you to dinner tonight? Repay you?"

"Thank you, kindly, Franklin, but I have so much to do. My daughter's coming on Friday, you see. But I'll tell you what. Why don't you come around Saturday evening for some eggnog?"

"Done," said Franklin. He headed off downstairs, and Dewey heard the front door slam and the roar of his bike.

Feeling only moderately guilty, she proceeded to inspect the rest of the bedrooms. The other two spares had an unused look like that of the dining room; but Victor Salgo's own bedroom was something else again.

It was jammed with furniture, for one thing. There were two bureaus, an enormous king-sized bed, a stationary bicycle, an enormous television, a stereo framed by a massive collection of CDs, and two bedside tables piled high with newspapers, magazines, unwashed coffee cups and glasses, and other detritus of the single male's life.

Dewey reproved herself for generalizing. She was quite sure that not all single men had bedrooms like this. She would bet, for example, that George washed out his coffee cups and put his newspapers in a neat pile.

She felt no compunction at all about going through Salgo's belongings. After all, she more or less had a mandate from the Board of Trustees to get to the bottom of things. Well, more or less—but that was all the encouragement Dewey needed. Having seen the kitchen, she now was certain that Victor Salgo had not taken his own life.

She opened bureau drawers and searched through the socks, flipped through address books, read small pieces of paper, looked at stacks of photographs tucked away in the bedside drawers.

So absorbed was she in her perusal of the man's life that the sound of the front door opening and closing nearly escaped her. She was on the point of calling out, and then thought better of it. Footsteps were heard mounting the stairs; Dewey, feeling ridiculous, plunged under the bed.

From her vantage point there was little to see, and soon she berated herself for choosing so unwisely. She was tucked well into the middle of the area under the bed so that she wouldn't be seen; with her cheek pressed flat against the floor, she got a sideways view of only one small area. A pair of sneakered women's feet moved toward her; it was impossible to see more than foot, ankle, and the lower part of the calf. Whoever it was had small feet, anyway; Dewey could see at a glance that they were not larger than a size seven, maybe even a six and a half. The legs were clad in some kind of khaki trousers.

Even if she couldn't see much, Dewey could pretty well figure out by the noises what was going on.

The visitor knew exactly what she was looking for, apparently. Without hesitation she pulled out the drawer of the night table and rummaged around. A muttered oath? Something. More rummaging. Then a trip around the foot of the bed to the other night table. More searching.

Now the legs moved over toward the bureau. From this wider angle, Dewey could see the khaki trousers all the way up to the knee. She could hear the visitor shift the little boxes and picture frames and doodads on top of the bureau, then pull out the drawers one by one. No luck. The other bureau was given the same treatment. Then there came a pause, as if the person was thinking things through. A hurried search through the piles of magazines on the night table; a quick look in the bathroom, and then the feet came back through the bedroom and out the door.

Dewey realized that she had been holding her breath. She let it out slowly, feeling the adrenaline rush of fear. She waited under the bed for what felt like hours, until she heard the front door open and close again. A look at her watch showed that it had been nearly half an hour since the arrival of the visitor.

Still nervous, Dewey slipped out and made her way on hands and knees to the window. She raised her eyes slowly to the level of the sill and looked out, but she could see nothing.

Whoever it was had come and gone on foot, and probably through the woods, just like Dewey.

Trembling a little, and aware of an achy stiffness in her knees and back, Dewey sat down on the edge of the bed.

It was only then that she realized she was still clutching something in her hand: a small leather-bound diary, about two inches by three, with onionskin pages.

No wonder the visitor hadn't found what she was looking for. Dewey had had it with her under the bed.

"Ye gods," she said aloud. "Curiouser and curiouser."

15

"FIELDING BOOKER," SAID Dewey, jabbing insistently at his desktop with her finger, "have you considered the possibility of murder?"

Booker, exasperated but momentarily lacking the zest for a confrontation, nodded. He was flipping through a manila folder, the fruits of his extensive interviews at the post office. There was nothing in his notes that could help those kids. Those toys were lost. "Murder. Yes, I have considered it frequently, Dewey. But I'm afraid they'd catch me. Besides, who would feed your horse for you?"

Amused by his own wit, Booker permitted himself the first smile of the day. Dewey ignored his joke and pursued her argument.

"Bookie, seriously. That man was murdered."

"Dewey, please. It's Christmas. Can't you find

a little of the Christmas spirit in your heart and *leave me alone*?" He glowered at her.

"I'll be happy to, Bookie, once this little problem is cleared up. Listen. Here are the facts." And she related the facts—the strangeness of the anonymous letter to the Board of Trustees and the suddenness of Salgo's disappearance, his having borrowed Franklin Lowe's guitar and his failure to turn up for the Winter Pageant, the oddness of his having rented a car, the wine and cheese, everything. Or nearly everything. She didn't mention the visitor to Salgo's house, or the little diary, whose contents had left her nonplused. At first glance, the diary didn't seem valuable at all; not even interesting. But Dewey knew it was of interest to someone.

Booker waited impatiently for her to finish her litany of anomalies, and then he gave her a look of utter disbelief. "Dewey, you know what? This time you have flipped. The man had an accident. Tragic, but these things happen. Perhaps he was drunk."

"Bookie, how can you say such a thing? I really thought you could put your personal pride aside for once and listen to reason. But no—you just make up your mind, and refuse even to consider the evidence. When it's right before you. I think you're prejudiced, Bookie."

Booker's eyes flashed merrily: He had an ace in the hole. In spite of his confidence, he had done a little checking. He hated it when Dewey came to him brandishing facts he didn't already know, and had long ago found it wiser to be well informed. Now he leaned back in his office chair, a satisfied smirk on his broad features.

"You always think you're one step ahead of me, but you're not. We haven't dilly-dallied about at the police station. We have given sufficient *professional* consideration to the circumstances. We have spoken with the car rental people. Mr. Salgo was to have turned the car in at the Cincinnati airport on Friday night. He had a plane reservation to Miami with further booking to Grand Cayman, where he had reserved a suite in a hotel for ten days. Now, what do you make of that?"

"Smoke."

"I beg your pardon?"

"Smoke, Bookie. It's all a smoke screen." Dewey leaned forward, intent. "Anybody can make a plane reservation, or a hotel reservation. Had he purchased the tickets?"

"No, but—"

"Had he paid for the hotel?"

"No, but a fax had been sent, confirming the dates."

"Bookie, even *I* can send a fax. I could book you a room in Timbuktu right now, but that doesn't mean that you intend to go."

If Booker was troubled by the possibility, he didn't show it. "But you see, Dewey, he did mean to go. He had a suitcase in the car with him; he was on his way."

"He was driving to Cincinnati?"

"Doubtful. Presumably he intended to catch one of the puddle-jumpers."

"But he didn't have a reservation." Dewey was triumphant.

"That doesn't mean anything. Lots of people don't make reservations. The flights are canceled half the time anyway."

Booker had a point. The Hamilton airport, like so many small airports everywhere, had been strategically located at the nadir of a gigantic, gentle depression, into which fog—if there was any for fifty miles—instantly crawled and settled, sometimes for days. Dewey herself never made a reservation on the commuter airlines; she just checked the weather report and headed to the airport.

"Was there fog predicted for Thursday night?"

"Who said he was flying on Thursday night? His flight to Miami wasn't until Friday night."

"Aha!" said Dewey.

"Aha, nothing."

Dewey had to change tack. Booker was meeting her every thrust with parry. Finally she found a chink. "Bookie, what was in the suitcase?"

"What you'd expect, Dewey. Clothes."

"Yes, but what kind? Bathing suits, shorts, shirts, all the right things?"

"Dewey, we saw no reason to—"

"Where is the suitcase?"

"It's being held. Until notification of next of kin."

"Well, then, Bookie, perhaps you'd be kind enough to let me take a look at it."

"Dewey, your imagination is working overtime."

"Did he have his passport with him?"

"Passport." Booker's voice was flat. Did the man have his passport? He couldn't remember. He furrowed a brow in thought, and then grew angry with himself. He was falling, as usual, into Dewey's trap. Well, this time, Fielding Booker wouldn't bite. This time, Dewey James was not going to lead him up the garden path of gossipy speculation. There were sixty-three disabled children in New York City who were *not* going to be denied a Christmas. Not if Fielding Booker could help it. Dewey was only getting in his way.

"Dewey, I have work to do. I won't discuss this lunacy with you further. I'd appreciate your going, now."

"Very well," said Dewey, without rancor. Booker would come around, she knew. But he lacked a little in the imagination department, and so it was frequently up to her to connect the dots for him. Once this had been done, she simply had to sit back and wait for the picture to take shape clearly before the good police captain's perplexed gaze. "By the way, I'm expecting you on Saturday. Grace will be here, and we'll have eggnog in the parlor."

"Bah, humbug," retorted Booker. But he would be there. Dewey knew that he would come.

She slipped out into the cold winter air, just as Officer Kate Shoemaker came bundling up to the front door of the police station. The two women stood on the steps outside and exchanged a quick hello. Kate held up a manila envelope. "Was it the ancient Greeks who killed the messenger, Mrs. James?" she said ruefully.

"Bad news?"

"He'll think so." She gestured with her head. "That's all that counts."

"Well, chin up, my dear. In spite of his temper, he's really a very fair man."

"That's easy for you to say," said Kate with a smile, and she darted inside.

Mike Fenton was sitting in front of a rickety old typewriter in the outer office, poking away with two fingers.

"Hey, Mikey," said Kate. "Want me to do that for you?"

Fenton turned around and glared at her with suspicion. "What's up?"

"Nothing. I just thought you might want my help. I'm better at typing than you are."

"And not half as good at conning people."

"Okay, be that way." Kate tried not to show her disappointment. One of these days she would get Mike to take the bait. He was infuriatingly good at ducking Captain Booker's wrath.

He read her mind. "Oh, in case you have anything to report, watch your step. The old man's in a temper because Mrs. James was just here."

"Yeah, I saw her on the way in. What's she onto?"

Fielding Booker's subordinates were respectful, obedient, and hardworking. But they had a conspiratorial fondness for Dewey James, and when she went to the mat with their captain, they often cheered for her behind Booker's back. Well—not to mention the fact that she was so often right about things.

"She's been giving him an earful," said Fenton, "about the guy that died in that rental-car crash. Salvo, whatever his name was.

"Salgo?" said Kate, trying to keep her voice even. "What did she say?"

"That we'd better investigate, because the guy was murdered."

"That woman is amazing," said Kate.

"Well, she likes to be useful, I guess."

"No, Mikey, that's not what I mean." She tapped the manila envelope. "Bob Gaston's medical report. Preliminary examination shows that the victim of the crash was heavily sedated."

"Sedated? Or he'd had a few?"

"No. He was zonked out on barbiturates. No way, says the doc, that he could have been driving moments before the crash. Based on lividity, blood content, who knows? All that stuff. He couldn't have driven the car down the ravine. No way. He was passed out."

"Jeepers creepers, Katie." Mike shook his head and turned ostentatiously back to his typing. "I don't envy you this one. He'll blow sky-high."

"You rat fink," said Kate Shoemaker.

16

WHILE FIELDING BOOKER was finding out the bad news, Dewey was searching for a motive. It seemed too simple to be true, the diary with the onionskin pages. And if it seemed so, it probably was. But Dewey was going to study it anyway.

It had few entries—it wasn't full of social events or little notes about parent-teacher conferences. But there were initials, followed by checkmarks, about every two weeks. It made no sense to Dewey.

Many years ago, serving an internship during her graduate study in library science, Dewey had worked as a school librarian. She had been young and inexperienced at the time and thus probably thin-skinned; but the memory still rankled. It had been a very unpleasant experience, because of all the political backbiting at the school (a small private institution in an eastern city). Dewey, still fresh from the cocoon of her education, was amazed to see with what spleen and bitterness the teachers and administrators had quarreled amongst themselves and put each other down.

The reasons soon became clear: Administrative changes were imminent, and everyone was anxious. Now, Dewey thought back to that experience. Then, as with the Jefferson, insecurity in the administrative system, in the power structure, had turned the school into a breeding ground for jealousy, acrimony, and malice.

A situation like that also spawned gossip of the vilest sort, and some of it would be true. Without further need for reflection, Dewey decided that her next visit would be to the Jefferson School itself. Franklin Lowe had been grumbling about a special meeting of teachers and administrators that had been called for this afternoon, presumably to tell everyone what everyone already knew. Dewey climbed in her car and drove out the four miles along the Rumson Road to the big, imposing, beautiful Jefferson campus—there to engage in espionage, eavesdropping, and hear what the rumor mill had to say.

The Blair Building, a three-story Greek Revival structure almost in the plantation mode, looked especially impressive today, in the cool wintry sunlight. The grounds had been planted long ago with beautiful copper beeches, hemlocks, oaks, and elms; only a single elm remained, but the other types had flourished, giving the main approach to the school a parklike atmosphere.

Dewey parked and walked around through a series of porticos to the brand new auditorium, which had been inaugurated only last semester with the drama society's production of *Oliver!*. Tommy Reynolds had only a small part, but by all accounts he performed magnificently. Dewey felt certain that if detective work should ever prove dull, the theater would be waiting for him.

There were about four hundred students at the Jeff, Dewey reckoned; faculty and staff totaled about eighty. Of these, Dewey estimated that she knew about half. It was unlikely that they would all turn up today, and if they did no one would question Dewey's presence. She was often invited to come to the school as a guest speaker for reading projects and library assignments; she was a familiar figure, and could be said to have a legitimate interest.

Leticia Sanderson was waiting quietly beside the podium, watching the staff trickle in. Despite her evident desire to be in control, she looked harried, almost spooked. Dewey knew her slightly and didn't like her very much, but decided that perhaps it would be worth saying hello, at the very least, after the meeting.

Most of the teachers sat in little clusters—by department, it seemed, or perhaps by grade. The secretaries and maintenance people kept to themselves, staying well over to the right. Dewey recognized Walter Hartung, the crusty old head custodian.

It had been a long time since she'd seen him, and she was surprised to find that he still worked at the school. For many years he had occasionally moonlighted at the library, helping to move stacks or repair things or lay carpet; but eventually Dewey had grown tired of his perpetual crankiness. Walter seemed to think he was the only person in the world who was ever tired, or overworked, or underappreciated. She wondered why the Jefferson had tolerated him so long; on the other hand, he was a whiz with everything from plumbing to wiring to the logistics of moving furniture. If he had learned to smile every now and then, he might have done great things. Dewey made a mental note to talk to Walter; he was sure to have a lot to say. Dewey had sometimes thought he hoarded facts about people.

"Thank you all for coming," Leticia Sanderson began. "I know it's an inconvenience, especially this week, when many of you have family obligations. And I know you are probably still tired from last term." A rumble of agreement swept the crowd. Leticia held up a hand. "Most of you, anyway, already know why we're here.

To discuss, in a frank and open forum, the sudden and very tragic death of our former headmaster, Mr. Victor Salgo."

There was a murmured response from the staff. Clearly, most of them had heard the news.

Leticia Sanderson went on, rehashing the bare facts: that Salgo had died in an accident, when the car he was driving went off the road and plunged into Johnson's Ravine. That the police were satisfied that it was nothing more than an accident; and for this reason, Leticia was here to plead with them on behalf of the school and the community not to engage in idle speculation, rumors, and gossip. There was the school to consider.

Well, thought Dewey, that was like the old mind-game, when you tell someone, "Quick! Don't think of a pink poodle!" There was no faster way to fan the fires of idle speculation, rumor, and gossip.

The woman was up to something. Either that or she was extremely stupid, and Dewey didn't believe that was so.

Leticia's homily went on for a few moments longer, and then she took questions from the audience. The main question everyone wanted answered—How long would Leticia Sanderson be filling Salgo's shoes?—was something no one had the nerve to ask.

There was a memo of some kind that was handed out to everyone at the close of the meeting. Dewey made sure she got a copy, stuffed it in her huge handbag, and went off to buttonhole Walter Hartung.

On her way down the aisle she passed Murray Hill, who gave her a grin. "Hiya, Mrs. James."

"Dewey, please," said Dewey.

"I'm sure looking forward to your little gathering on Saturday. Is there anything I can bring?"

"Just bright spirits. Listen, Murray—I must dash, but I want to talk to you. Are you busy? Can you wait for me somewhere?"

"Sure, in my office in the Huber Building," said Murray. "The old red-brick one. Room twelve."

"Thank you. I'll be there in fifteen minutes."

Dewey hurried along. Walter's pace had been slowed drastically by rheumatism, or perhaps by age, and Dewey felt a momentary surge of regret at her unkind recollection of the man. But when she caught up to him and tapped him gently on the shoulder, he turned and glared at her; so maybe her feelings about him were on the mark after all.

"Excuse me, Walter?"

"Howdy."

"Howdy yourself. How are you?"

"Tired, bone-tired. Aching. Don't you come begging for me to come round to that library of yours, Mrs. James. No way. I'm a tired old man, and you're too cheap."

Dewey steered him gently out of the auditorium and into the hall next to the lunchroom. The crowd thinned, and most of them, moving faster than Walter could, passed them by. There was relative privacy.

"I haven't come to ask you to help at the library. But I did come for your help. Where can we talk in private?"

"In here." Walter gestured to the lunchroom door and took a massive jangle of keys from his belt. With practiced fingers he slipped them by until he found the right one, opened the door, and then shut it again behind them.

The lunchroom was lit only by the ghostly illumination of four or five Fire Exit signs that perched over every door. The whole room was bathed in a pinkish glow, but Walter apparently didn't find it odd, since he made no move to turn on the overheads. They seated themselves in a booth along one of the walls, and Dewey began.

"What do you think happened to Victor Salgo, Walter?"

"I think he finally got what was coming to him."

"Murdered?"

"Damn straight. He had it coming." Walter pulled a pack of Old Golds from his pocket and lit one. Dewey didn't know anybody still smoked, much less smoked Old Golds. She stared at the pack.

"Want one?" Walter gestured.

"No, thank you. I've just promised my daughter I'd give it up," lied Dewey. She had never smoked in her life, but she didn't like telling that to smokers. It made them defensive. "She's a health nut, but if I want any peace, I have to go along with it."

"Kids," murmured Walter Hartung, shaking his head sorrowfully, as if to say, What stupid things would they get up to next?

"Why did he have it coming to him?" Dewey was back on track.

"Because, number one, he was two-timing about six different women, or maybe three-timing them. Number two, he was lettin' the school go down the toilet, excuse my French. Number three, he had some little girl back in New York City suing him for harassment. And number four, he was blackmailing a couple of people around here."

"Good heavens!" Dewey sat back, amazed. "Those are some strong assertions."

"Assertions, hell. They's facts, Mrs. James, and there's a pile of people here who know most of 'em. But maybe old Walter's the only one who knows *all* the facts."

Dewey didn't have to wonder why Walter knew all the facts. He was everywhere and nowhere—the kind of person that people tended to ignore or overlook altogether. The kind of person who could hang around a doorway with a mop, listening to a telephone conversation, without raising much suspicion.

Dewey knew better than to forget that Walter might eavesdrop. But then, Dewey thought of him as a whole person, not just as a mop and a pail.

"Well, Walter. Let's say he had it coming to him. Can you elaborate on that statement?"

"Well, the women, for starters. There was one that he used to hang around with a lot, a pretty little thing, but older than him. I think he got tired of her. And of course there was Vivian, but that weren't serious, and Vivian don't hold a grudge. She goes with everyone. Then there was one of the mothers. Lady called Hatch, Hatched, something. She and him was an item when he was just a teacher."

The list of women didn't sound too promising; it seemed to be nothing more than a succession of girlfriends. "How about the harassment suit? Was that something that could be solved easily?"

"Sure—all he had to do was pay up. I used to hear him talking to his lawyer about it, arguing. Lawyer didn't want him to pay up, wanted him to fight it, because otherwise the school's in a heap of you-know-what, makes it look like he's guilty."

"And was he?"

"Mrs. James, the way I sees some of these so-called little girls behaving, it's a wonder they

don't get their little behinds sued right off 'em,
or put in jail to cool down. So maybe he took
one up on her offer. That's not a crime."

"No, but it's not very seemly behavior for the
headmaster of the Jefferson."

"Yeah, but he wasn't head of nothing back
then, only a plain and simple old math teacher.
Notice how the girl didn't sue until he's big and
important and he can make her rich."

"Yes," agreed Dewey, not finding it hard to
believe. "And speaking of blackmail . . ." She
let her voice trail off.

"Yeah, well, now you're talking bad," agreed
Walter. "Don't nobody hold with that. We all
aren't perfect, need to have our sins corrected
and forgiven, not sent to us in the mail, marked
payment due."

"Walter, can you tell me who might have been
involved?"

Walter scratched his head, coughed, and
reached for another cigarette. "Not for sure.
Nope, but here's what it looked like to me—
only my opinion, you understand." Dewey nodded. Walter, in other words, had no proof of
what he was about to tell her.

"You know that lady done give a good speech,
but every person in that room knows she's a
mean one. Only cares about herself. Everyone's
afraid of her, except this boy come here from
New York City, and he goes toe to toe with her
all the time. Before him, I knew what a bad act

she was. I wasn't never afraid of her. She's just mean. But old Victor, he had something on her. She was scared of him."

"Right from the beginning?"

"I think. I remember she cut up rough when they started talking about making him head of the school. Well, a lot of folks did, but you know how that goes. Anyway, she gets ready to get all the teachers to put their names on a piece of paper, saying he's not right, but then suddenly she stops that idea and shuts up. Never said a word against him after that. But look where she is now."

Dewey had to admit that Walter had a point. *Cui bono?* She wished him a Merry Christmas, but he only grunted. Then she meditated on his revelations all the way to the Huber Building, where Murray Hill was waiting for her.

"Shakespeare believed in watching out for people like Walter," said Murray Hill, when Dewey had told him a little bit about her conversation with the custodian. "His characters were always being done in by living messengers and spying servants. Pivotal, some of them, at least to the action and sometimes in terms of characters' relationships."

"It doesn't ever do," agreed Dewey, "to ignore people or be scornful of them."

"What exactly did Walter tell you, anyway, Mrs. James?"

"Just that Salgo had a lot of enemies. Is that true?"

"I wouldn't have used the word *enemies*," Hill responded. "But it's true that nobody liked him." He gave Dewey a shrewd look. "Mrs. James—you think Victor Salgo was murdered, don't you?"

Dewey nodded. "Oh, I think so, Murray. Quite definitely."

"Then I suppose 'enemies' isn't too strong a word."

"Why did nobody like him?"

"Hard to say. He was abrasive, but lots of people are abrasive, so it wasn't that. But he had a way of— I don't know how to put it. Of making use of people and then discarding them. When you do that, people start to dislike you."

"Do you think it possible that Salgo might have been blackmailing someone?"

"Yikes!" Hill thought a moment. "I wouldn't have put it quite that way, but you know, I think it might be possible."

"Hmmm," said Dewey. "That's what Walter thinks."

"But let's remember, Mrs. James, that there are all kinds of blackmail, not just the kind for money. And as for Walter, who knows what level of information he's actually familiar with." Hill grew thoughtful. "Victor Salgo was an anomaly; he didn't fit the role he'd been thrust into here at the Jeff. So people were insulted, or jealous, and they went around making up reasons for his success: He was a blackmailer, he was a token, he was a Don Juan—whatever worked for your particular grudge. Sounds like Walter's got a multifaceted case of hostility, which could be the source for a lot of the speculation."

"I suppose that's one way to look at it," replied Dewey. "But I've known him a long time. He's always been a sourpuss and a crank, but I haven't known him to spout off like that before."

"No—besides, I think he has a point."

"Why?"

"Because all the powerful people around here were trying to get rid of Salgo—but nothing overt. They couldn't be seen to be working against him."

"Because they were afraid?"

Hill shrugged his shoulders. "It makes sense, doesn't it?" Murray told Dewey about his having been enlisted by Rigton Blair to make sure Salgo didn't come back. "Funny thing, though. I'm not a hundred percent sure Blair didn't just want me to stir up some kind of campaign. I think he wanted Salgo out of commission."

"I don't like the looks of this situation, Murray. I certainly hope that it can be cleared up before the end of the winter vacation, for the good of all concerned."

"What do the police think, Mrs. James?"

"Er, the police, I'm certain, will soon be exploring every angle. No doubt Captain Booker will want to talk to everyone involved."

"Why, thank you, Dewey, for setting the stage so nicely." Fielding Booker's voice boomed across the little office.

Murray Hill raised an eyebrow. "Can I help you?"

"Well, now, young man. Let me see. Are you Murray Hill, of"—Booker consulted a piece of paper—"one-oh-five Normandy Place?"

"That's me," said Murray.

"Well, then. I'm Captain Fielding Booker, of the Hamilton Police. But I think you know that. Would you be so kind, sir, as to come along with me?"

"Bookie, what *are* you—"

"Hush, Dewey. Police business." He cocked an eyebrow at Hill. "Are you coming?"

"Of course. Wouldn't miss the excitement for anything." He pulled on his coat and said goodbye to Dewey. "Mrs. James, would you be good enough to lock the door behind you? Thanks ever so."

17

DEWEY KNEW FIELDING Booker well enough to know that he was trying to get back at her for being right, and that he would use every trick in the book to get her goat. Unfortunately, he was succeeding. But she was firmly resolved not to let it bother her. She hurried home and put in a call to George.

"George, that *idiot* Bookie is arresting the nice young man from the Jeff. Just when I've got him coming for eggnog with Grace."

"Whoa, Nellie," said George soothingly. "Who's coming for eggnog with Grace? The young man? Or Bookie?"

"Murray Hill, of course. Well, Bookie, too—of course, too," said Dewey, more jumbled than usual. "But after the way he behaved this afternoon, maybe not," she added ominously.

"I wouldn't let it worry you, Dewey." George was soothing. "After all, you've spent the last two days digging up evidence of a crime and prodding him to get involved. You can hardly hold it against him when he takes your advice."

"Well, he doesn't have to be so uppity." Dewey was becoming mollified.

"Sure he does. He's got his pride, remember."

"He's not likely to let me forget it. Why does he want to go and arrest Murray Hill, George?"

"He's not arresting him, Dewey. Here's what happened. Booker got the medical examiner's report, and guess what?"

"It said that Victor Salgo was murdered."

"Got it in one. How did you know?"

"George, everyone knows. Even Walter Hartung."

"That old complainer? Well, if he knows, then I guess it must be true. But Booker is a man of science, or something. So now it's been medically demonstrated to his satisfaction." George told Dewey about the barbiturates found in Salgo's system. "Bob Gaston called me on it. Knew I was on the board, God knows how, and thought I ought to be told. I'm beginning to feel like the heart and soul of the Jeff."

"Never mind all that, George," said Dewey. "Why is Bookie arresting Murray Hill?"

"He's not. He's only questioning him as a material witness."

"Why?"

"Because of that package that was in the door one day and gone the next."

"Oh." Dewey had forgotten about the package. Booker hadn't. One up for him. "Well, I'm glad he's decided to investigate, finally."

"I don't think he has much choice, Dewey, after receiving the report from Doc Gaston."

"No, I suppose not. Well." Dewey was silent a moment, thinking; then George interrupted.

"Dewey, don't you think you've done enough? You can leave it to Bookie from here. After all, if it hadn't been for you, nobody would have known."

"If it hadn't been for Tommy Reynolds, you mean." Dewey sighed. She would have much preferred it if Fielding Booker occasionally co-operated on a case. But he left her no choice. "Never mind, George. I've got to dash. Errands to run." She hung up, and less than two minutes later she was upstairs tugging on a pair of jeans and boots. She had managed the whole thing up to now, but Bookie was always going off half-cocked when he got himself in over his head. She wasn't going to let Fielding Booker blow this thing sky high.

There was still a full two hours before it would be getting dark. Realizing she hadn't had any lunch, Dewey grabbed a cheese sandwich as she went through the kitchen out the back door. Her Christmas decorations, which she had planned to put up today, would just have to wait. She saddled Starbuck and headed off through the countryside, up Adams Hill and down through the woods bordering Leithdown Farm. She was bound for Rigton Blair's country estate.

Clyn Malira sat at the top of a long, sloping hill. It had been the seat, originally, of the Greaney family—Charles Greaney, one of the founding fathers of Hamilton, and his son William, who had designed and owned the original canal system for the Boone River, thereby turning the family's modest fortune into a truly monumental pile of cash. Rigton Blair was somehow descended, on his mother's side, from the Greaneys—she had been the niece of the grandson of a half-sister, or something like that. His father's family, the Blairs, were Johnny-come-latelies compared to the Greaneys; but the Blairs were very, very, very rich, so that made up for a lot. The Blairs had bought the Greaney estate about half a century ago, just as the Greaneys ran out of money. Dewey had heard that it had gone for a song.

Oh, well. Bankers often got bargains, but that was all right, Dewey supposed. Blair National Bank had bankrolled plenty of projects in and around Hamilton over the century it had been in business, and nobody really paid much attention anymore to the stories of how the first Blair had got the money to start a bank. That was ancient history—the brothel had long since been razed to the ground, and the statute of limitations had run out.

Dewey didn't actively dislike Rigton Blair. He was a fixture in the town, and although he had never been particularly generous toward the library—actually, for a millionaire, he had been downright stingy—he was after all deeply involved in education through the Jefferson; so she supposed they had a lot in common. She supposed.

On the other hand, she had never been able to work up more than a feeling of distant cordiality for the man. He was a cold fish if ever there was one, and Dewey had heard (as one heard such things) that he was a difficult person to work for, constantly finding fault with his employees, and generating on the whole a sense of insecurity and suspicion among them. He had wide acquaintance but few friends, and he had never married. In short, thought Dewey, as Starbuck cantered up the grassy hill that led to the house, he was "as secret, and self-contained, and solitary as an oyster."

The ride from her place to Clyn Malira had taken no more than half an hour, since Dewey knew every shortcut, and Starbuck, despite her advanced age, still enjoyed taking the occasional fence. Dewey had rehearsed a little speech on the way over, having to do with what a beautiful day it was for a ride, and she hoped Mr. Blair wouldn't mind too much if Dewey prevailed on him for a drink of water before moving on.

She was in luck: Rigton Blair was at home, or at least his Mercedes was parked in the porte-cochère around the side of the grave house. He often left the bank early in the afternoon, Dewey knew, lunching at his club and not returning until the following morning. She tied Starbuck to a branch of an old apple tree in a side yard and made her way around to the front of the house, her boots crunching on the gravel of the driveway.

Dewey's footsteps must have been audible at a considerable distance in the quiet that sat like a pall over the Clyn Malira estate. She was surprised that there were no dogs to liven the place up; it didn't seem right for a house this large to be without at least one unmannered springer spaniel, and a cranky old cocker to bite unsuspecting children. But she supposed that Rigton Blair had as little use for dogs as he did for people. It must be a little on the lonely side, this place.

Dewey rang the bell and waited; a sour-faced aproned maid eventually arrived at the imposing wood door and gave Dewey a suspicious look. "Yes?"

"Mr. Blair, please. I'm Mrs. James."

The maid did not reply, but stood aside and allowed Dewey to enter, and then disappeared, leaving Dewey alone in the enormous entrance

hall. She removed her riding hat and wind-
breaker and looked around.

The hall was large and welcoming, with wide-
plank wooden floors and beautiful Chinese rugs.
The hall ran all the way back to another massive
door at the opposite end of the house. It's length
was broken by a staircase midway down, and
four sets of double doors, two on each side. A
quick glance to her right showed Dewey a small
dining room, beyond which she guessed was the
kitchen. She peeked through another set of
doors: a large, formal dining room. Too bad
Rigton Blair had never been one to entertain.

Across the hall, a third door led to a formal
living room, whose furniture had a distinctly
unsat-in look; the fourth pair of doors led to a
small library, beyond which another door opened
into a billiards room.

Dewey wondered, not for the first time in her
life, why wonderful places like this were wasted
on the people least likely to enjoy them.

The maid came back. "You can wait in here,"
she said, gesturing to the library. Dewey stepped
in and began to look around.

The room was lined on three sides with
floor-to-ceiling bookshelves. Dewey was impressed by the quality of the collection: rare
books, an elephant folio of Audubon prints,
calf-bound sets by a single author, slim volumes
of poetry, and a wide assortment of what looked

like diaries, photograph albums, and yearbooks. Some of them looked familiar to Dewey. There were only a few jarring elements in the room—the television, a modern, swivel-type easy chair in black vinyl, a set of folding tray-tables, and a stack of brightly bound paperbacks on one of the bookshelves. Idly, Dewey read their spines: Lawrence Sanders, Tom Clancy, Ken Follett, Robert Ludlum. So Rigton Blair was human after all.

On the shelf in front of her were works of American authors: Twain, Sinclair Lewis, Hawthorne and Melville, Fitzgerald, Hemingway, Mencken. She pulled a few out and opened to the title pages: first editions, the lucky man. Dewey looked with special longing toward the Fitzgerald—a first edition of *The Great Gatsby* must be worth quite a lot of money, she reasoned. She picked it up and opened to the flyleaf. "To RB, for all our memories of those bright college days!" No signature, but presumably Blair knew who had given it to him. Next to the Fitzgerald, which except for the inscription looked untouched, was a moth-eaten copy of *The Snows of Kilimanjaro*; Blair apparently preferred Hemingway to Fitzgerald, which somehow surprised Dewey.

"Afternoon, Mrs. James." Dewey started. Rigton Blair had entered the library silently. "Sorry they haven't got nice little numbers on their backs for you. Have a seat." He gestured to a small, worn armchair, and plonked himself in the modern vinyl thing. "Suppose you tell me what you're here for." His cool gray eyes were emotionless.

"Good afternoon, Mr. Blair. I was just out for a ride, don't you know, and thought I'd prevail on you for a glass of water."

"Poppycock."

"Er, that is, my horse is tied up out in your orchard. I hope you don't mind."

"Don't give a damn about your horse. Do care why you turn up on my doorstep. Don't get me wrong, Mrs. James. It's not to say you wouldn't be welcome here under the proper circumstances. But I know you better, perhaps, than you think I do; I know your reputation as well. When Dewey James comes calling unexpectedly on people that she doesn't really care for—"

"Now, Mr. Blair—"

"Hear me out, woman. When you go dropping in on casual acquaintances, you are always after something. It's not time for the annual fundraiser for your library, and besides you know you'll get damned little from me. Don't like lending libraries. Cater to the hoi polloi."

Dewey suppressed the urge to glance toward the stack of thrillers. She merely glowered at Rigton Blair, and he went on, oblivious or immune to her mounting ill temper.

"So I ask myself: What's she come here for,

that woman? If she doesn't want money, then it's ten to one she wants to stick her nose into somebody else's business. Now, what is there on my plate that she could possibly want to pick away at? Not the affairs of the bank—not even Dewey James is forward enough to try to get something confidential out of me. So it's got to be the Jefferson School. So here I am, ready to head you off at the pass. The concerns of the Jeff have nothing to do with an old busybody like yourself. So I suggest you take your meddlesome ways and be gone. The only reason," he added, dropping his final words into Dewey's astonished silence, "that I even came downstairs to see you was to make sure that my message to you was delivered in no uncertain terms. There are too many timid souls about, Mrs. James, who think it's a crime to speak plainly to people. I am not one of them. If you've come prying and spying and snooping, then you are not welcome here, and I will not discuss the affairs of the Jefferson School with you."

"I see," said Dewey brightly. She gathered up her hat and her jacket. "I'm glad you're unafraid to speak plainly, Mr. Blair. That very characteristic means that you certainly would not have been one of those unfortunate timid souls whom Victor Salgo was blackmailing." She flashed him a smile; he didn't respond, but sat frozen in his chair. "Because had you been a timid soul, Mr. Blair, unafraid to speak plainly, then instead of telling Salgo to go to blazes, as you have me, you might have knuckled under to his extortion. Which would make you not only a timid soul but, *ipso facto*, a suspect in his murder. I bid you good day, Mr. Blair."

Before the old crank had a chance to get himself up out of his swivel seat, Dewey was gone. Her heart was still pounding mightily as she mounted Starbuck and galloped furiously down the long hill, away from the house. Dewey hauled left on the reins and Starbuck whirled, headed at full speed for the fence that separated Clyn Malira from the pastures at Leithdown Farms. The fence was a high one, but Dewey urged Starbuck on. Starbuck, ever willing, was up, up, and over—coming down with a bit of a thunk on the other side. The mare regained her balance and galloped with her mistress, all the way home.

18

BACK AT HOME, Dewey felt unready to tackle the Christmas decorating. She made herself a strong cup of tea, fed Isaiah his supper, and sat down in the kitchen to think.

Cui bono? To whose benefit was it that Victor Salgo was dead? Dewey reached for an old envelope and a ballpoint pen and made a list.

Leticia Sanderson: She was the most obvious, thought Dewey, because she was now Acting Head of the Jeff, which had been her chief goal. Also, if you believed Walter, Salgo had represented some kind of threat, not just to her ambitions but to her livelihood. The petition that had been withdrawn. Blackmail?? Dewey made a note to talk to her tomorrow.

Rigton Blair: Strictly speaking, Dewey wasn't sure he benefited, but he certainly had wanted Salgo out. Long before the murder, he had been angling for a way to fire him before his term was up. Dewey wondered, Could Blair produce the anonymous letter charging Salgo with being "a thief and worse"? And what kind of situation had Salgo been facing with respect to the young woman from New York City? Dewey had nothing to go on but rumor.

Walter Hartung? Dewey didn't want to ignore him as a possibility. Why had he been so willing to criticize Victor Salgo? Was it possible that Walter had an axe to grind?

The telephone rang, and Dewey paused in her meditations to answer.

"Dewey? Thank God you're there. It's Margaret Reynolds."

"Whatever is wrong?" asked Dewey, with a sinking feeling.

"Dewey, is Tommy with you?"

"No, he's not. I haven't seen him since yesterday, when we went to see Fielding Booker."

"Oh, God."

"Calm down, Margaret," said Dewey firmly.

"Dewey, I can't think where he could be. He's just impossible, that boy. He promised me he would be back by dark, and it's almost six-thirty, and no sign of him."

"Did he go on his bike?"

"Yes. Listen, I thought maybe you would know. If you hear anything, please call."

"Yes, of course, Margaret," promised Dewey, and hung up.

The call bothered her. Margaret Reynolds was not the type to become alarmed at the drop of a hat. Dewey reproached herself severely: She had been careless. She had been so proud of Tommy that she had bragged about his finding the license plate. Had she also bragged about his having seen a light in the woods the night before?

Because surely, Dewey thought, her flesh tingling, that light had belonged to Victor Salgo's murderer.

"Oh, dear heaven, Isaiah," said Dewey. She reached for the phone in a panic and called George.

If the truth be told, there was nothing George Farnham liked better than being necessary to Dewey James. For several years she had been necessary to him, in a way that he hadn't dreamed would be possible after Lois died. Maybe, just maybe, Dewey was coming around. There were occasional signs of it; and George—faithful, patient, and kind old George—was content to wait. While he waited, however, he did what he could to advance his cause. Tonight, Dewey needed him. Feeling like Sir Lancelot, he leaped into his car and sped out to her house, to hold her hand and help her figure out what had happened to her young friend.

When he got there, he was a little disappointed to be handed a bowl full of cranberries and popcorn. "We might as well do something useful while we wait," insisted Dewey, who was not particularly good at tasks like stringing cranberries and popcorn, and certainly not above taking advantage of the willingness of others. "Here, George, here's the needle and thread. You do it, while I get the garland." She disappeared and came back five minutes later with a huge length of pine garland. "We'll wrap the cranberries and popcorn string around the garland, and then the whole thing can hang from the valences in the parlor."

"If you say so, my dear," said George amiably, poking the needle through a cranberry.

Dewey put a tape of Christmas music into her little stereo system and sat down on her worn, nearly sprung red velvet sofa. She was now prepared to worry in earnest. It had been a half hour since Margaret's call, and Dewey had just tried the house. So far, no Tommy. "George, I feel utterly responsible. But we will find him and bring him home safe. We just have to use our deductive powers to think of where he is. Then we can rescue him. So. Where do you think that boy could be?"

George liked the music and the homey task before him, but he preferred the role of Sir Lancelot. He was feeling a little deflated. "Well, at a guess, Dewey, he's playing at a friend's house and forgot to clue his mother in. You said you think she's overprotective."

"Yes, but she has a right to be worried. It's dark outside, and he's on his bicycle."

"Maybe he had a flat tire and had to walk the bike home."

"I don't think so. You have to put yourself in the mind of that boy. I'll bet you he's investigating another clue somewhere."

"What kind of clue, Dewey? There aren't any."

"That never stops little boys. Little girls, either."

"Big girls, either," said George, with a twinkle in his eye.

"Never you mind. So. If he's investigating, where do you think he would go?"

"Hmm. The car-rental company."

"No. They're closed."

"School."

"For what?"

"Well, how should I know? To spy on the headmaster's office?"

"No. Besides, it's vacation. Why would a boy go to school during vacation?"

"You've got a point, Dewey."

"How about the house of the victim?" Dewey, with a sudden sense of certainty, dropped the Christmas garland and reached for her jacket.

"Whoa, whoa! How would he get in?"

"He'd find that spare key in a minute, George."

"I suppose you're right."

"Suppose the person came back—the one who was searching the house when I was there?"

George dropped the string of popcorn and cranberries. "Let's go, Dewey."

They drove the half mile to Victor Salgo's house. As they drew near, Dewey looked through a stand of pines. There was a faint light shining upstairs somewhere.

"Probably a night-light in the bathroom," said George, ever practical.

"Or a flashlight. Tommy's flashlight." Dewey turned off the engine and the headlights and let her car drift to a stop. "George," she admonished in a whisper, "don't forget that we're dealing with a cold-blooded killer."

"I won't forget," came George's whispered response.

They closed the car doors as quietly as possible and walked on the grass along the driveway. When Dewey reached the front stoop she tried the door gently. It opened noiselessly. Dewey gave George a frightened look and tiptoed on inside.

They stood very still in the darkened front hall, listening. From upstairs came a firm, reproachful voice, but Dewey couldn't make out the words. Every now and then the voice would stop, and then start up again, as if waiting for an answer from an interlocutor.

Quietly, they crept upstairs. There was a faint

light coming from underneath the closed door to one of the spare bedrooms. Now Dewey could make out the words, and she recognized the voice as well. She had heard that voice only this afternoon.

"You are going to be very, very sorry, young man. Do you understand?"

There was a muffled response. Dewey, her heart fluttering, felt a rising panic. She looked with wide eyes at George. They had nothing with them, not even a stick or a can of Mace.

Dewey thought fast. Then she hurriedly whispered her plan to George, who tiptoed down the hall and into the next bedroom.

Dewey, meanwhile, crept downstairs and out the door. Then she rang the doorbell, loud and long, and jiggled the doorknob for good measure.

It was a few moments before she heard anything. Then a light went on in the little library, and footsteps approached. The outside light was switched on, and the door opened a crack.

Leticia Sanderson stood on the threshold. "Yes?"

"Oh, Ms. Sanderson, forgive my barging in like this," said Dewey in a loud voice. "But you see, my car has stopped dead out there, and I wondered if I might use your telephone."

Leticia hesitated, then swung the door open. "It's in the kitchen," she said, "on the wall—"

There was a boisterous shout from upstairs. "Mrs. James!" yelled Tommy Reynolds, bounding from the stairs.

"Well, hello there, Tommy," said Dewey, playing it cool. They weren't out of the woods yet. Where was George?

Leticia gave Tommy a black look, and the boy approached more casually. "I—uh"

"Good heavens, Tommy, look at the time, would you?" exclaimed Leticia. "Thank you *so* much for coming to visit—that was very nice of you. Why don't you run along, then."

"I'll take you, Tommy," said Dewey. "Go call your mother and tell her you'll be home soon."

Leticia turned swiftly at the sound of a footfall on the staircase. With a sharp intake of breath, she wheeled on Dewey. "What is the meaning of this? What is George Farnham doing upstairs in my house?"

"More to the point, Leticia," said George, as he reached the bottom step, "what are you doing here?"

"I'm entitled to be here."

"On whose authority?"

"George, am I or am I not Acting Head at the Jeff?" She didn't wait for an answer. "Is this or is this not the headmaster's house? Or, should I now say, headmistress." She looked defiantly at George, who stared back at her in mild confusion. Either this woman was the most tactless and ambitious individual he'd ever met, or she was a born actress. Or perhaps both.

"Leticia, don't you think it would be a good idea for you to wait for the board's approval before moving in here?"

"Who said I was moving in, George? But I did come over to get a few things. File folders out of the library. In case you think I'm taking it easy over the vacation, I'm not. There's a great deal to be done. A great deal."

"I see."

"And when I got here, I found that young whippersnapper on the premises, if you can believe it."

She shot a glance toward the kitchen, where Tommy was conversing with his mother in a loud, cheerful voice. "I'm with Mrs. James, Mom," he was saying. "What could be safer?"

"I didn't see your car out front, Ms. Sanderson," remarked Dewey.

"No—I walked over. The exercise is good for me."

"Well, how about you let us take you home," suggested George. "I wouldn't want you out there wandering around in the dark. You might get hurt."

"All right," said Leticia, with bad grace. "Just let me go and get those files out of the library." She came back in a moment with several folders tucked under her arm, and the four of them drove to Tommy's house. Before he climbed out of the car, he gave Dewey his solemn promise to call her in the morning.

"Leticia, I think we need to talk, freely and frankly," said Dewey, when they had seen Tommy safely indoors.

"I can't imagine why," said Leticia, but her tone wasn't as mulish as her words.

Without waiting for Leticia's consent, Dewey pulled into her own driveway. Isaiah came to the door to greet them, gave Leticia a suspicious sniff, and then followed the threesome into Dewey's parlor.

The half-strung cranberries and the pine garland lay where Dewey and George had left them; the place looked anything but Christmasy, thought Dewey.

Leticia, at Dewy's invitation, sat down on the red velvet sofa; George went off to the kitchen and came back a few moments later bearing a tray with sherry, Scotch, and three glasses. While George was gone, Dewey took a good look at Leticia's feet. Probably at least an eight-and-a-half; maybe a nine. They were not the feet Dewey had seen from her hiding place under Victor Salgo's bed.

This didn't surprise Dewey. Because that visitor had searched the house quite carefully from top to bottom, looking for something. Whereas Leticia, the instant she scented trouble, had gone straight to Salgo's library and removed two manila folders. Leticia didn't have to search. She knew where to find what she wanted.

Leticia had been like a zombie since Tommy got out of the car. Now as George offered her a drink she sat up a bit, accepted a glass of Dry Sack, and sank back into the comfort of the sofa.

Dewey looked her over carefully. The woman's expression was a perpetual scowl; her demeanor was overbearing. Yet tonight, she seemed tired, worn out—and all of a sudden vulnerable.

"Leticia," began Dewey gently, "I don't know if you've heard this news. The police have evidence that Victor Salgo was murdered."

"Impossible," said Leticia, her spunk returning. "He drove off a cliff, that's all."

"Do you know why anybody would want to murder him, Leticia?"

"Hah. Who wouldn't have? I'm almost sorry it *was* an accident. He was a monster, a horrible, dreadful man. Dreadful."

"Leticia, I have it on good authority that you were being blackmailed by him."

Leticia Sanderson looked wide-eyed at Dewey and gulped her sherry. "Could I have a refill, please, George? Thank you." She sipped, and regarded Dewey once more. "What a ridiculous idea."

"I don't think you were the only one, Leticia. Blackmailers are generally repeat offenders, especially when they are successful the first time around. But he knew something about you, didn't he? That you didn't want anyone in Hamilton to learn."

"That's absurd, Dewey."

"Is it?" Dewey reached quickly for the manila folders that Leticia had taken from the library at Salgo's house. She opened one at random: in it were old newspaper clippings from a small weekly published on the North Shore of Boston: IPSWICH WOMAN DENIES DRUG CHARGES, read one headline. LOCAL GIRL FACES JAIL IN NY UNDER ROCKEFELLER MEASURE, said another. Behind the clippings was the photo that Dewey had seen in Salgo's house of a group of young people at a rock concert. The girl in braids and Indian-print cotton was a much younger, much happier Leticia Sanderson.

"This is what he was using to torment you?" asked Dewey, trying to keep the disbelief from her tone. "This?"

Leticia sat like a stone. George took a look at the materials in the folder and shook his head.

"What happened, Leticia?"

"It was all a mistake." Her voice was monotone. "I wasn't even there at the party when the police made the bust, but one of my so-called friends had borrowed a jacket of mine. It had my name in it. It also had her bag of hashish. I arrived about ten minutes later, and there were the cops, and I thought maybe there had been an accident or something. Then someone said, "There she is," and one of the cops said, "This yours, lady?" And I thought he was giving it back to me, being nice. So I said yes, thank you, and reached out for it, and he put the cuffs on me, and that was the end."

"Surely you could have proven your innocence," suggested George. "Any good lawyer—"

"Any good lawyer, George, costs money. I had no money, and my father refused to help me, and so I went to jail for a year."

"Oh, dear." Dewey's voice was sympathetic.

"It's not the kind of experience you ever get over, either. Not if you're a sheltered little rich girl from the North Shore, used to yacht clubs and parties and having whatever you want."

"No, I suppose not," agreed Dewey.

"The other inmates hated me. They beat me up, stole everything I had, shaved my head, tore up pictures of my boyfriend—you name it. It was only a year, but it was a lifetime, and I came out a different person."

"But how on earth did Victor Salgo dig this up? And why?"

"The why is easy—he wanted money and power. I don't live very well, maybe, but I am the only daughter of very wealthy parents, now deceased. My father never forgave himself for what happened to me, because he could have prevented it, but he wanted me to learn a lesson. So he threw money at me the rest of my life to try to make up for it, but the money doesn't help. It doesn't chase away the nightmares, and I don't enjoy it. So Victor Salgo was welcome to it."

"Yes, but, Leticia—how did he find out?"

"He knew I had a secret—you know there are people who can always tell when someone's got a dirty little secret. I'm one of those people. So was he. So he did some digging—I never changed my name or anything, and he just did some plain old research into my past. It wasn't anything very difficult to do."

"And he threatened to tell Rigton Blair?"

"He threatened to tell the entire board, the town, the world. I just didn't want it dug up again—I couldn't stand it. I never got over my anger at being tricked that way, and I never really forgave my father, either, although I tried." Leticia drank the last of her sherry and stared straight ahead. "Now you know, and soon the whole world will know. The only thing in life I've ever really cared about, besides the Jeff, was burying that time. But I've never succeeded."

"Nobody needs to know," said Dewey kindly.

George raised an eyebrow. "Dewey, how—"

"You leave all of that to me, George." She dismissed his worries with a wave. "Leticia, if you want to help us find Salgo's murderer, you can."

"Now, why on earth would I want to do something like that?"

"For the good of the Jeff?" suggested George.

"Or maybe because, without your help, the wrong person might go to jail for a crime he didn't commit," said Dewey, in a voice both soothing and stern.

19

Armed with the facts about Leticia Sanderson, Dewey felt much better. The poor woman had suffered greatly, and there was no reason why anyone needed to know about it. On the other hand, being privy now to Leticia's secret made it easier for Dewey to do some further investigation into the blackmailing activities of Victor Salgo. Dewey was convinced that there were more victims here, and it was very likely that one of those victims would prove to be the murderer.

The next morning Dewey paid a visit to police headquarters, where Fielding Booker was in a mood of high jollity. He was resplendent in an ancient double-breasted pin-striped suit, with a magnificent high collar, a marroon cravat, and a matching silk handkerchief peeping coyly from his breast pocket. He looked a little like Al

Capone, thought Dewey. But only a little. It was the pin stripes.

"Top of the mornin' to ye, Dewey," blared Booker. "Come round to be useful, have you?"

Dewey was always wary of Booker's high spirits. They usually came at her expense. "What's going on, Bookie?"

"Well, Dewey, I know that you think we of the Hamilton constabulary are very inefficient. Plodders, if you like to characterize us so."

"I've never said that," retorted Dewey.

"Sometimes one does not need to *say* a thing, Dewey," Booker replied ponderously. "One sometimes communicates without *saying*. For example, by taking the law into one's own hands."

"I have no idea what you mean," protested Dewey innocently.

"Balderdash. Balderdash and flummery. But be that as it may, Dewey, I am inclined to share with you the fruits of our labors. Because you are a relatively law-abiding member of our little community, after all, and you are constantly expressing interest in the workings of the great Mandala of Justice."

Dewey began to wonder if Booker were drunk. But she had never known him to overindulge— for him, it would be a crime on a par with wearing blue jeans or a collarless shirt. Not thinkable. She decided to play along.

"All right, Bookie. Clue me in. I am prepared to be amazed by your judicial wizardry."

Mike Fenton stuck his head in at Booker's office door. "All systems go, sir, for Operation Hoover."

"Operation Hoover?" asked Dewey, trying not to giggle.

"Code name, Mrs. James. I'll fill you in later." With a wink, Mike was gone.

"Shall we, then, Dewey?" Booker took his gray cape from its hook, donned a soft felt cap, and took up his walking stick. He bowed Dewey out the door, and she—mystified, amused, and intrigued—was happy enough to tag along.

"You see," said Booker, as Kate Shoemaker drove them out along Rumson Road, Dewey and Bookie in the back, Mike Fenton riding up front, "it wasn't a matter of fancy footwork, but good, old-fashioned, professional police procedure. We went to the rental agency and showed them a picture of Victor Salgo. And do you know, the girl at the desk swore up and down, left and right, and a hundred ways to Sunday that Salgo was not the person who had come in to pick up the car."

"Oh, no?" said Dewey, not surprised. If he had been passed out on barbiturates, it was quite likely that it happened at his house—in which case he wouldn't be in any shape to drive, let alone pick up a rental car. And if his "trip" to Florida and Grand Cayman was all a ruse concocted by the murderer, then why would he have gone to pick up a rental car at all? "It wasn't Victor Salgo?"

"No." Booker permitted himself a small smile. "But here's the really interesting little twist. I asked her—she's just a wee little thing, not more than nineteen years old, and you know how unreliable girls are—"

Dewey, who knew no such thing, let it pass. This was interesting.

"Anyway, I asked her how she could be so sure. 'Well, to start with, sir, I think you got the wrong rental party,' she said to me."

"The wrong car company?"

"No—the wrong 'rental party.' She dug through her files and found the signed copy of the contract. And guess who signed it?"

"V. Salgo."

"Yes!" exclaimed Booker. "Not Victor. V. Salgo. You see my drift? Perhaps not. The wee little girl behind the counter says, 'It was a lady what rented the car.'"

"I don't suppose she knew *what* lady," prompted Dewey.

"Not her name, of course. But she did give us a full description. Mikey?"

Fenton pulled a notebook from his jacket pocket, flipped it open to the appropriate page, and read the girl's statement aloud:

"'I don't know about height and stuff, but I know the lady had kind of grayish-blond hair, curly, and glasses. No makeup. She was wearing a blue blazer with brass buttons, one of those button-down shirts like men wear, and a tan skirt. Boots.'"

Uh-oh, thought Dewey. There had to be a way to salvage this disaster. Her mind raced, only half aware of Booker as he prattled merrily on.

"Hah, hah!" chuckled Booker. "Dewey, remember, please, that going *by the book* will always get you there in the end. Now, who does that sound like to you? To me, it's obvious, but then I'm a police officer, trained to notice small details. Ring a bell?"

"Bookie, I hate to tell you, but—"

"No? Well, then I'll tell you. But first, a lesson in detecting, since you're so eager. Remember— when you're faced with a homicide, always ask, Who gains from this? Nine times out of ten, the murderer is going to be the person who stands to gain the most. Now, I ask you. Who gains? And, more to the point, who wears a tan skirt, button-down shirt, and blue blazer *every day of the year*? Whoops—too late. We're here."

Kate Shoemaker pulled the car into the small driveway in front of Leticia Sanderson's house. "Mike, you and I will go in and cuff the suspect. Kate, you remain outside in case she decides to make a dash for it. Dewey, for God's sake don't get in the way of our operation."

Dewey thought desperately. She could hide in the trunk of the police car, or disappear into the woods, or face up to the situation like a brave person. The one thing she knew she would not be able to do was dissuade Booker from his present course of action.

She knew in her heart that she couldn't run away. Reluctantly she stepped from the car and stood next to Kate.

When Leticia opened the door, she looked as though she hadn't slept. Her eyes were puffy and her hair was unkempt; but she was dressed in her regulation blazer, skirt, and shirt. Dewey wondered briefly if it was Leticia's stay in prison that had convinced her of the vanity of trying to dress well. Why bother, when your whole world can fall apart at a moment's notice?

"Good afternoon, Miss Sanderson," said Booker, his tone icy and forbidding.

Leticia's face drained of what little color it had. Spotting Dewey behind Booker, she called out, "Dewey, what is this?"

"It's all a misunderstanding, Leticia—" Dewey began, but Booker hushed her.

"Official police business, ma'am. I'm afraid I'm going to have to ask you to come with us."

"What ever for?"

"In connection with the murder of Victor Salgo."

"Are you arresting me?"

"We'd like you to come with us, ma'am," said Booker flatly.

Dewey could see it all in the woman's face. The last time Leticia had received a similar invitation from a policeman, her life had changed forever. She wasn't about to play the fool a second time.

"Show me your warrant," she said, "and then I'll call my lawyer."

"Very well." To Dewey's dismay, Booker produced a warrant, freshly signed by Judge Baker.

Leticia turned her back on them. "I'll just call Tony Zimmerman," she said. "The telephone is upstairs. I won't be a minute."

Dewey felt the panic rising. "Bookie, you will regret this!" she said fiercely. She followed Leticia up the stairs and into her small bedroom.

The woman had opened the top drawer of her bureau. Now she turned on Dewey with a pistol in her hand. "It's not going to be used on you, Dewey. Don't worry. Although I must say you deserve it."

"Leticia, it's a misunderstanding. Listen! Someone is trying to frame you."

"Yes—someone called Dewey James."

"No! Leticia, I promise—I had no idea about this. This is all Booker's doing. Well, you know how he is. Bullheaded."

"What's going on up there?" shouted Booker from below. "Mike, go on upstairs and make sure that James woman doesn't get any foolish ideas."

"Yessir," said Fenton, climbing the stairs two at a time.

He froze in his tracks when he saw the gun. "Um, Miss Sanderson?"

"*Ms.* Sanderson, Sergeant. Booker is a fool, but you're young enough to learn. *Ms.*"

"Can you put that thing away, please? It might go off."

"That, I believe, is the whole idea of guns," said Leticia, with a glint of unwonted humor. "That they should go off."

"Leticia—Mike." Dewey was desperate. "This is all a dreadful mistake. You can help me straighten it out."

"Uh-oh," said Fenton. He gave Dewey an appraising look and dropped his voice to a whisper. "The old man making another bloomer, Mrs. James?"

"Yes, I'm afraid so. Please, Mike. We can straighten it out."

"Please put the gun away, Ms. Sanderson," whispered Mike. "If Dewey James says you're innocent, then you're innocent. But play along for a little while, will you?"

"You're asking too much," said Leticia bitterly.

"Half an hour, Leticia. Then everything will be all worked out."

"And if it's not?"

"I'll go to jail with you," promised Dewey.

Dewey drove like a speed demon all the way from police headquarters to the car rental office.

George had come rushing over from his office at Dewey's urgent request, and was now standing guard over Leticia, interfering mightily with the great Mandala of Justice, as spun by Fielding Booker. With the entire police force of Hamilton working on the Salgo case, Dewey figured that she wouldn't get a speeding ticket.

It took no little convincing, but Dewey finally managed to pry the "wee little girl" from behind the desk, promising the manager to return with her in less than an hour. Dewey did not talk to her on the way over lest she be accused of influencing the testimony of a witness. All she said was that it was a matter of life and death. And this was no exaggeration.

"What the devil?" spluttered Booker, as Dewey and the young clerk—whose name, Dewey found out, was Vanessa La Reina—gate-crashed the little party in the interrogation room.

"I just thought it would be simpler," said Dewey, with a smile, "to get everything on the record right away." She looked at the girl. "Vanessa? Do you see in this room the woman that rented the car from you that night?"

Vanessa looked from Leticia Sanderson to Kate Shoemaker and back again. "Nope."

"NOPE!?" bellowed Fielding Booker. "*NOPE??!!*"

"Well, you wouldn't want me to lie, would you? You got that lady"—she pointed to Leticia—"all dolled up to look like her. But it ain't her. Not even close. The lady what rented the car, she dint look like her. Only the clothes is the same."

"Thank you, Vanessa," said Dewey with authority. "Officer Shoemaker will drive you back to work."

"Now, you just wait a ding-bangled MINUTE!" shouted Booker, pounding the interrogation table with his fist. "Dewey James, you have got NO right to interfere in the legitimate workings of justice. None."

"I agree, Bookie," said Dewey. "When you've got legitimate workings of justice going on in this place, I'll be the first to congratulate you. Let's go, Leticia."

"Blast that woman," said Booker. "George, can't you do something about her? Train her, tame her, teach her some manners? Get her to behave."

"Oh, I doubt I could, Bookie," said George with a smile. "But you know, I kind of like her the way she is. If it ain't broke, don't fix it." George bowed a farewell and ducked out into the cold December air.

20

"WELL, WE KNOW it wasn't Leticia Sanderson, George. Who does that leave?" They were on their second cup of coffee at Josie's Place, having polished off a piece of pie in short order. The little restaurant was jampacked with Hamiltonians laden with gifts, bags, mufflers, and hats, and the holiday spirit. It had been almost impossible to find a table, but finally a booth had opened up.

"Vivian the Vivacious?" suggested George. "Remember that Walter said Salgo had recently thrown her over."

"Walter also said she doesn't hold a grudge."

"The girl from New York City."

"The mother of the girl from New York City."

"More likely," George agreed. "Vanessa said it was a lady not a girl."

"Maybe it was a man."

"Rigton Blair in drag? I doubt it. It's not his style."

"Maybe not. But you know, I think Salgo was blackmailing him, too. Maybe we can get him to open up."

"Maybe." George wasn't hopeful. "What do you think Salgo had on him?"

"I'm just guessing, but I think it has something to do with his record in college. Where did he go to school, George?"

"Harvard, of course. Would Rigton Blair go anywhere else?"

"Probably not. I went to see him the other day, you know."

"You didn't! My dear, you take my breath away. You are so intrepid!"

"Well, he huffed and puffed and blew my contrivances down, George, but I think I rattled him. And I saw something out there that should have given me a clue, but I was so busy being impressed by Clyn Malira that I didn't really have the presence of mind to think it through. So. Come with me to the library while I make a phone call."

"Splendid idea, Dewey. Absolutely splendid." George signaled for the check, put four dollars on the table, and away they went.

"Yes, this is Mrs. James calling from Hamilton," said Dewey, using her politest voice. "I'm the chief librarian here, and we're putting together a little local history, a sort of *Who's Who in Hamilton*. I wonder if you could help me. I need to know what year someone graduated. Rigton Blair. B-L-A-I-R. Yes, I'll hold."

George was sitting in Dewey's visitor's chair, his feet on her desk, enjoying her end of the conversation. Dewey could be very persuasive when she chose to, and she worked absolute miracles, as a rule, with bureaucratic types.

"No?" said Dewey, her eyes lighting up. "Forty-nine, I would guess, perhaps forty-eight. No? But I know he entered. From the Jefferson School, class of forty-five."

She talked a few more minutes, then hung up. "The Alumni Office has no record of his graduating, although he entered."

"Call the registrar," suggested George. "They'll tell you."

"Even better," suggested Dewey, "I'll call one of his classmates. Billy Mott. Do you remember him, George? Stubby, wonderful sense of humor, knew everything about everyone. Lives in Connecticut now, grew rich on the stock market in New York."

"Ye gods, Dewey, how do you keep it all straight?"

"I'm a librarian, George. A fact-filer by nature."

Twenty minutes later Dewey and George were at the Blair National Bank. "Tell him it's Mr.

Farnham, on urgent Jefferson business," said George to the secretary/watchdog who guarded the inner recesses of the banking floor.

"And her?" asked the secretary, pointing to Dewey with a red-lacquered talon.

"This is Mrs. Huffington Duke, who wishes to see Mr. Blair personally. She wished to make a sizable contribution to the school's endowment," said George magnificently.

"Okay. Wait a minute." The secretary jabbed at a button, spoke into the phone, and waved them through.

Dewey knew that as long as she lived she would relish the memory of that moment. George entered the office first, and Dewey lagged behind a few steps. Blair, all cordiality when the scent of money was in the air, rose and greeted George heartily. "And Mrs. Duke?" he said, in a gentle, eager voice, looking around hopefully. "You've brought Mrs. Huffington Duke?"

"Unfortunately," said Dewey, making her entrance, "Mrs. Duke was unavoidably detained, so she sent me in her place."

Rigton Blair turned ashen-gray, and looked from Dewey to George and back again. He began to quiver, and then he sat down firmly in his chair. "I didn't expect this sort of thing from you, George."

"Probably not," said George, casually taking a seat. "But then again, I knew you'd tell

Dewey—a neighbor, and one of the pillars of our community—to get lost before she had a chance to have her say. But Mrs. Huffington Duke, whoever she might be, is always welcome. Is that right?"

Blair looked chagrined, but he didn't respond.

"Because her name has money in it," added Dewey. "I'll just talk for a moment or two, Mr. Blair. It may please you to know that I'm not a timid soul, and speak plainly."

"Oh, do shut up and get on with it," said Blair. "You tiresome old woman."

"I'm younger than you are. Only by a year or so, it's true," Dewey amended, "but there is that year. My husband was just your age."

"The cop."

"Yes, if you like. The cop." Dewey saw no need to take up the cudgel, although George bristled. "He and you were classmates, did you know? At college."

"I don't remember him," said Blair. "But I'm sure he wasn't in the Porcellian, and I really don't mix outside the club."

"No, he wasn't in the Porcellian," agreed Dewey. "They don't have a Porcellian Club at Bay State Community College."

"Ah—is that where he went? G.I. Bill and all, I suppose. Your error, Mrs. James. We may have seen each other on the train, heading East, but that would be all."

"Really? Even after you were expelled from

Harvard for cheating, and registered at Bay State under a false name?"

"What? That is the most absurd allegation—"

"Oh, come down off your high horse, Blair," said George sternly. "Dewey just got off the phone with Billy Mott. He told us everything we wanted to know."

Rigton Blair seemed to crumple. He looked from Dewey to George and back again. "So you've decided to hold me up, have you? Get something from me, because I was once a stupid young man?"

"Oh, not at all, Mr. Blair," replied Dewey gently. "We only thought it might do you some good to talk. We think Victor Salgo extracted enough of a price from you for his silence."

"I am very glad that monstrous man is dead," said Blair bitterly.

"But you will be a suspect in his murder," said Dewey, "as I warned you the other day. It would be much better to let us clear up any little misunderstanding, before the police turn it into a bigger one."

"Yes," said Blair, a defeated man. "You win, Mrs. James. Well." He rose. "It won't do to talk it over here. Shall we go to my club?"

"I'd rather not," said Dewey. "How about the library? It's private."

"If you insist."

*   *   *

"He was bleeding me dry, that man. He was going to make it impossible for me to leave money for the Jeff. I would have loved to kill him. But I didn't."

Dewey produced the little diary that she had taken from Salgo's house. "He recorded your payments. Are these thousands?" She showed him the book.

"Tens of thousands," said Blair. George whistled.

"Well, what did he do with all that money?"

"He had a numbered bank account in the Cayman Islands, like all the other crooks in the world."

"So he *was* going to Grand Cayman!" said Dewey.

"Oh, I don't think so. He had planned to take a vacation there, with that dreadful woman friend of his, but they had some kind of falling out. I gather she was getting greedy."

"How so?"

"Well, she knew he had a pile of money. And she wanted to get her hands on it. Salgo told me, laughing, that he didn't want a greedy girlfriend. He wanted a generous girlfriend."

"So they broke up."

"Oh, yes. He laughed about it. I think he had been rather cruel to her. She was older than he, you see, by a good ten years, and he made quite a lot of that."

"But, Rigton," said George. "Who? Who was the girlfriend?"

"Oh, sorry. Thought everyone knew. That horrid woman that sits on the Jefferson board, George. Sandra Albee."

21

"I FEEL RIDICULOUS," complained George. "Bookie, are you sure this is necessary?"

"Absolutely, George. You never know when a woman's going to open up to you. If we can get it, we'll use it."

Mike Fenton and Kate Shoemaker were encircling George's midriff with adhesive tape. She and Mike had both seen a lot of movies in which people wore wires, so they had an idea, more or less, of how to go about it. Somewhere under all the layers was Kate's portable tape recorder. She wasn't sure how well it worked, but the batteries, at least, were fresh.

Dewey was sitting in a corner, giggling. "I hope she doesn't try any funny stuff while you have that thing on, George. Heaven knows what she'll think of all that tape holding you together. You don't look *that* old."

"Aw, Dewey, that's not fair," pleaded George, beginning to laugh himself. "Ooh, don't make me laugh! It pulls out the hair on my chest!"

After their discussion with Rigton Blair, Dewey and George had gone into a deep huddle, from which they emerged with a plan to trap Sandra Albee—either by obtaining an incriminating admission or getting Vanessa, the car-rental clerk, to identify her. The two plotters agreed that George would make the best bait; they also decided, however reluctantly, that Fielding Booker would have to be called in professionally. "We can't bypass him altogether, George," Dewey had pointed out. "Somebody has to make an arrest, after all."

So George had phoned Sandra and invited her to dinner. No public meeting at the Seven Locks this time, but a dimly lighted corner table at Luigi's. Dewey, it must be said, was feeling a little bit jealous, since Luigi's was sort of their special spot for romantic dinners. George, however, was a sensitive man, and he promised not to order any of their favorite dishes, which made Dewey feel better.

Needless to say, it had been Booker's idea for George to go wired. Oblivious to the nice distinctions among electronic devices, he had obliged Kate to surrender her little personal tape recorder to the cause. Well, thought Dewey, watching them put the finishing touches on George's midsection, Bookie deserved to have a hand in the planning. He was, after all, the captain of police.

"Hurry up, you two," urged George. "I've got to pick her up in fifteen minutes."

"You're all ready, Mr. Farnham," said Kate, giving his back a slap.

George put his shirt back on, tied his tie, donned his jacket, and was on his way—moving a little funny, Dewey observed, but moving.

"Now, here's the plan," said Booker, in a voice like thunder. "Mikey and Kate, in plainclothes, will be at the next table. Try to make it look romantic—Mikey, your wife will just have to understand. I'll come around eight o'clock with our witness. If it's a make, get out the cuffs." Booker eyed Dewey. "You. Home."

"No, sir," said Dewey. "Either I go with you or I go on my own. But this is my, er, bust, Bookie."

"Dewey, you'll blow George's cover."

"I doubt it," said Dewey. "I'll be as discreet as a potted plant. Scout's honor."

"All right. You come with me." He grabbed the roll of adhesive tape and brandished it at her. "But one word, and I'll use this on that mouth of yours. I swear to you."

They swung by the car-rental office and picked up Vanessa, who by this time was beginning to relish her role as star witness. She had dressed for the occasion—a tight-fitting ribbed brown turtle-neck, a pair of freshly pressed jeans with holes at the knee (front and back), and new cowboy boots. Her young mouth glistened with rust-colored lipstick, and her nails were painted to match. She was quite a sight.

"Don't know what gets into young girls," muttered Booker, disapproving.

"It's only fashion, Bookie," Dewey assured him. "Pay it no mind; it's all transitory."

"I suppose so." He sounded sad.

Booker drove cautiously out the winding road to the quiet little country restaurant, where Luigi tended lovingly to his patrons, like an overanxious gardener watching the progress of his orchids. He knew the best spot for each one, knew the best wines to serve them, and had a knack for smoothing over those unfortunate little to-do's that couples always seem to have in restaurants, rather than in the privacy of their own homes. Luigi had been clued in as to tonight's activity. When Dewey arrived with Booker and Vanessa, they were smuggled into the kitchen through a side door; in the main room of the restaurant, Luigi was laying it on thick for George and Sandra, laughing, twirling his mustache, and making suggestive little move-ments with his eyebrows.

Dewey strained to get a peep through the little round window in the swinging door between the kitchen and dining room. Harried waiters hustled past the intruders, their arms loaded to the elbows with plates. (Trays were a cardinal sin at Luigi's.)

When the traffic back and forth to the kitchen slowed a little, Dewey got a good glimpse of Sandra and George. The woman had her hand on the table and was drumming her fingers gently, laughing lightly at something George had said. George was smiling broadly. Dewey thought he was overdoing it just a bit. He didn't have to act like it was so much fun for him.

Now Sandra's fingers were inching their way across the table. Dewey, transfixed, was almost bowled over by a scurrying waiter, who made no apology, but just pushed past her. She watched in horror as Sandra Albee's red fingernails reached out and touched the back of George's hand, ever so lightly. "Enough, you harpy!" exclaimed Dewey.

Booker looked at her sharply. Then he brought Vanessa up close to the other swinging door. She *was* a wee little thing, admitted Dewey; Booker had to lift her so that she could see through the little round window. All it took, however, was one look.

"That's her," said Vanessa.

"Are you certain?" asked Booker, groaning under the strain of holding the wee girl up.

"Yeah, I'd know her anywhere. She almost made me lose my job."

Booker put Vanessa down and asked a passing waiter to give the signal to Kate and Mike. Scurrying past their table, arms laden with *gnocchi in brodo*, he nodded. Mike and Kate rose and approached Sandra Albee, who gave them a perplexed stare. Mike produced a piece of paper from his pocket and read it to her.

Sandra sat motionless for a moment. Then she stood up, took her plate of *fettuccine à la putanesca*, and poured it over George Farnham's head.

22

It had taken Dewey a full twelve hours to get over laughing. Every time she thought of George with that pasta all over his head, she collapsed anew in a fit of giggles. George had found it less amusing, but still he admitted that he had it coming to him. They both had to remind themselves that it was no laughing matter.

Vanessa La Reina's identification of Sandra Albee proved unshakable; for such a wee little thing, Vanessa turned out to be hard as nails, especially when she found out what was at stake.

"Hey," she had said to Dewey, "I'm gonna let some bimbo walk away from that? And me live with it the rest of *my* life? No way. Do I look like a nut?"

So Sandra was duly charged the next day, and bound over for trial. She was not granted bail because it was feared that she might leave the country. Two false passports and a suitcase full of cash had been discovered at her house. The police also found a large quantity of phenobarbital and the khaki skirt and blue blazer she had worn to impersonate Leticia Sanderson. And on a little piece of paper—later found to have been taken from Salgo's office, the night after she drugged him and pushed him over that cliff—was written the number of Victor Salgo's bank account in Grand Cayman. She had been all set—the only thing was, she didn't want to travel alone.

Even in the excitement over Sandra's arrest, Dewey still managed to get the Christmas decorations up, to fix up Grace's room nicely, and to get to the airport in time (no fog) to meet her daughter's flight. The two of them rushed home, then dashed out to get party supplies. Grace, accustomed to her mother's way of doing things, had arrived prepared for the usual hustle-bustle. On the way home from the airport Dewey apologized, but Grace merely laughed. "Mom, I'm only sorry you didn't wait to have your sting operation. I always wanted to see George go wired to a meet."

Dewey thought Grace looked marvelous— suntanned and healthy and happy. She had a very good job with a marine biology laboratory, and spent a lot of time playing with dolphins and whales, which no doubt accounted for her high spirits. Knowing all of this made Dewey just a little bit sad, because she would have enjoyed it if Grace came home to live.

On Saturday, Dewey was finally ready for her eggnog party. She and George had finished stringing the cranberries, and had draped the garlands, and George, with a gentle persuasiveness, had insisted on making the eggnog. (Last year, tragically, Dewey had used allspice instead of nutmeg.)

At six o-clock, people began to arrive. In the aftermath of the arrest, Dewey had called Rigton Blair and extended an invitation to him as well. To her amazement, he had cordially accepted, and he had taken the opportunity to pour out his heart, such as it was, to Dewey. He even admitted to having written the "anonymous" letter he'd read to the Board of Trustees in November. From now on, he promised, he was a reformed man.

The other guests were surprised to see him, but they were more astonished to see that he had brought Leticia Sanderson on his arm. Well, George wasn't astonished. He had suspected something along those lines, ever since Blair had warned him off of Leticia. Neither one of them was smiling, but both looked as if they might thaw, sooner or later.

At six-fifteen, Murray Hill arrived and greeted Dewey. He grabbed George's elbow and gestured across the room. "Hey," he whispered. "Who's the dish?"

George chuckled. "That's Dewey's daughter, Grace."

"Oooh." Murray's admiring gaze lingered on the young woman. Tall, suntanned, and with a smile as wide as all outdoors, Grace James was definitely a knockout. Murray moved in for a closer look. Dewey was suddenly glad she had been such a typical mother.

Franklin Lowe arrived, bringing both his banjo and his guitar. He knew wonderful bluegrass and jazz versions of a lot of Christmas songs, and his "Winter Wonderland" was always a crowd pleaser.

Tommy Reynolds arrived, with his mother and father. He shook Dewey's hand solemnly. "You did it, Mrs. James."

"*We* did it, Tommy," Dewey told him.

Fielding Booker arrived, looking tired but happy. He greeted Dewey warmly, and even remembered to congratulate Tommy for "helping us to get the ball rolling."

"Sure," said Tommy. "Hey, Mrs. James. Is there a reward from the rent-a-car?"

"You'll have to ask Vanessa," said Dewey, pointing across the room. "She knows everything."

Booker turned to Dewey, beaming. "You won't believe what's happened," he said.

"What's that, Bookie?"

"The toys. They've found the stolen toys."

"Oh, how wonderful. Where were they?"

"Incredible." Booker shook his head. "A real miracle, Dewey. They got mailed."

"You mean they were never stolen? They were in the mail the whole time?"

"That's right. But the people in the Post Office weren't expecting such efficiency, and so they were reported stolen. But they arrived at the orphanage in New York today."

"Will wonders never cease?" said George, coming up to join them.

"So tell us, Bookie. What happened on the case today?"

"Not much. I think Albee's getting ready to plead guilty, though. She hasn't confessed, but I think that will come in time. She's not used to life in a cell, and it's wearing her down pretty fast."

"I can imagine," said George, thinking of the makeup, the hair, the perfect clothes.

"So what happened?" said Susan Miles, coming up to join the crowd. "Dewey, they tell me you've done it again. Congratulations."

"Ahem," said George.

"Oh, you too, George. I heard you went wired."

"Er, yes—"

"Bookie!" exclaimed Dewey. "When do we get to listen to that tape? I'm dying to hear it."

"Why, um—" Bookie looked at George, who

was frantically shaking his head. "Why, Dewey, it's evidence now. I'm not so sure when it will be released."

"You don't have to release it, Bookie. You just have to let me listen to it. I'll drop by tomorrow."

"Tomorrow is Christmas Eve, Dewey," Booker objected.

"I'll make the time."

George drew a finger ominously across his throat and looked at Bookie pleadingly. "I'm sorry, Dewey," Booker said firmly. "That tape is off limits. Don't ask me again, please."

"Well!" humphed Dewey. "He doesn't need to get all uppity with me."

Rigton Blair approached, dragging Leticia with him. He'd had a few cups of eggnog. "Wonderful party," he said. He turned to Leticia. "May I present Mrs. Huffington Duke?"

Leticia laughed, and the two of them wandered away.

From across the room Dewey was watching Grace and Murray Hill, deep in conversation. San Diego was such a long way away; but what could Hamilton offer a young woman like Grace?

Then she saw Grace laugh at something the nice young man from the Jeff said, and she knew what Hamilton had to offer.

Franklin Lowe sat down on Dewey's sofa and began to play. He really was talented, thought

Dewey. Murray Hill started to sing, and before long, all of Dewey's guests were joining in.

She looked around. Where was George? Had he left without saying goodbye?

She went to the kitchen, and then out the door into the backyard. There was George, hands in pockets, looking up through the cold into the moonless, starry sky.

"George?"

"Here I am."

"Everything all right?"

"Just fine."

"What are you doing?"

"I'm making up my mind."

"Oh. About what?"

"I'll tell you tomorrow."